A FIELD GUIDE TO
Fantastical Beasts

A FIELD GUIDE TO

FANTASTICAL
BEASTS

AN ATLAS OF FABULOUS CREATURES,
ENCHANTED BEINGS, AND
MAGICAL MONSTERS

OLENTO SALAPERÄINEN

STERLING
New York

STERLING
New York

An Imprint of Sterling Publishing Co., Inc.
1166 Avenue of the Americas
New York, NY 10036

ISBN 978-1-4549-2094-6

Distributed in Canada by Sterling Publishing Co., Inc.
c/o Canadian Manda Group, 664 Annette Street
Toronto, Ontario, Canada, M6S 2C8

For information about custom editions, special sales,
and premium and corporate purchases, please
contact Sterling Special Sales at 800-805-5489 or
specialsales@sterlingpublishing.com.

Manufactured in China

10 9 8 7 6 5 4 3 2 1

www.sterlingpublishing.com

Designed by Lucy Parissi

CONTENTS

INTRODUCTION

Here be dragons…and vampires, pixies, poltergeists, goblins, centaurs, witches, hellhounds, and dozens more besides. Fantastical creatures, supernatural powers, lucky charms, and wicked spells have fascinated mankind for many thousands of years. In these pages you will encounter the world's most amazing, most fearsome, most devilish beings and beasts, from diminutive dwarves to the mighty Kraken, wise jinn to brainless ogres, industrious brownies to lazy satyrs, luck-bringing qilins to doom-bringing banshees, and friendly wizards to the elusive Loch Ness Monster. Here are the man-made and the heaven-sent, the immortal and the undead.

Some, like dragons, angels, and giants, are ancient—more ancient than we will probably ever know. Others are much newer entries to the mythical menagerie: Christmas elves have only existed since the 1850s and gremlins since World War I; leprechauns swapped their traditional red clothes for green ones in the early twentieth century; mummies only began cursing treasure-hunting explorers in 1923; and zombies only acquired a taste for brains as recently as 1985.

Thanks to folklore, fairy tales, and religious texts, most fantastical creatures have remained unchanged for hundreds or even thousands of years. Some, however, have gradually undergone a complete reversal of character. Unicorns were

once described as "the most furious beast," with the head of a stag and the feet of an elephant, fairies were known for stealing children, and elves were blamed for sickness and nightmares. Demons, to the ancient Greeks, were benevolent spirits and muses. The Greek sphinx, on the other hand, was a cruel monster, while its Egyptian forebearer was an emblem of nobility.

THANKS TO FOLKLORE, FAIRY TALES, AND RELIGIOUS TEXTS, MOST FANTASTICAL CREATURES HAVE REMAINED UNCHANGED FOR HUNDREDS OR EVEN THOUSANDS OF YEARS.

Nowadays we may be skeptical about the existence of some of these creatures, but all of them were at one point very much believed in and either feared or venerated—and many of them, like ghosts and the yeti, still are. The Furies were so feared in ancient Greece that even uttering their names was believed to invite their wrath. In the late Middle Ages, European monarchs would trade vast riches for precious "unicorn horn." In 1493, Christopher Columbus earnestly reported a sighting of mermaids in the Caribbean. Two centuries later, suspected werewolves and witches were still being burned at the stake on both sides of the Atlantic.

From Australia to America, Germany to Japan, the beasts and beings in this book are guaranteed to amuse and alarm, and above all to serve as a warning. Do you know why you should never pick up a lost comb, surprise a sprite, give unclear instructions to a golem, or invite a mysterious Eastern European count into your home? If not, read on. Better to be safe than very sorry indeed.

CHAPTER 1

FAIRIES & LITTLE PEOPLE

Beautiful, fragile, and ethereal, fairies and their diminutive counterparts are among the best loved of all fantastical creatures. They have a reputation for being kind to humans: house sprites will do your work for you, gnomes will weed your garden, and leprechauns are likely to lead you to a crock of gold at the end of a rainbow. But it's not all flowers and fairy dust: for every happy little helper there's a sinister goblin or gremlin lurking in the shadows, waiting to cause mischief, damage, or even death...

SNOW WHITE AND THE SEVEN DWARFS

As famous dwarves go, joint first place surely goes to Snow White's seven housemates: Doc, Grumpy, Happy, Sleepy, Bashful, Sneezy, and Dopey. The Brothers Grimm published *Snow White* in their collection *Grimms' Fairy Tales* to great acclaim in 1812, but in 1937 Walt Disney made them the subject of the world's first animated feature-length film. He was awarded an Academy Honorary Award at the 1939 Oscars—which was accompanied by seven miniature statuettes.

Dwarves

Cheerful and helpful, dwarves are as old as the Earth, but beware the dwarf who has turned his power to evil.

Dwarves are little, mountain-dwelling men—female dwarves are in short supply—traditionally associated with Germanic folklore, although their precise origin is unclear. Dwarves are invariably described as short, bearded, old, and rather ugly, albeit cheerful and wise.

One of the earliest written references to dwarves is in the *Poetic Edda*, a thirteenth-century compilation of Old Norse poems. One of them, "Völuspá," recounts the creation of the universe and everything in it, including dwarves, and lists the names of all the dwarves over six of its sixty stanzas—a catalog that was mined by J. R. R. Tolkien when he was choosing names for the dwarves in *The Lord of the Rings*.

The *Prose Edda*, a comprehensive history of Old Norse mythology written in the thirteenth century by Icelandic historian Snorri Sturluson, describes how the sky is held up by four mighty dwarves named North, South, East, and West.

RUMPELSTILTSKIN

Dwarves can be cheeky but are rarely malevolent, although Rumpelstiltskin is a notable exception. According to the German fairy tale, he appears one night to a miller's daughter who has the impossible job of spinning straw into gold, and offers to perform the feat in return for the girl's necklace. The next night he demands her ring. On the third night she has nothing more to give—but Rumpelstiltskin claims the right to take her firstborn child. Years pass, the baby is born, and sure enough Rumpelstiltskin appears. In desperation the mother strikes a bargain with him: if she can guess the dwarf's name, she can keep her child. Rumpelstiltskin is so sure of victory that he sings himself a gleeful song with the ill-advised chorus "Nobody knows I'm called Rumpelstiltskin"—which is overheard by the woman's messenger, resulting in the return of the baby.

Elves

Elves are variously described as Santa's helpers, mischievous imps, or wicked little goblins that bring illness, pain, and nightmares.

Although elves are often paired with fairies in the popular imagination, the two species of little people have historically had very different personalities. Like fairies, elves are nowadays depicted as small, human-like sprites that live in tree hollows and overgrown wild spaces. They have delicate features with pointed ears, and often wear green or red clothing. But elves were originally feared rather than sought out, due to behavior that was almost exclusively mischievous, if not downright wicked.

DARK ELVES

In Germanic and Old Norse mythology, elves were human-sized supernatural spirits with magical powers, which they used to bring about illness or other misfortune. In the thirteenth-century *Prose Edda*, Icelandic historian Snorri Sturluson describes the *Dökkálfar* (dark elves), who live underground and are blacker than black to behold. He also mentions a distinct species called *Svartálfar* (black elves), whom nineteenth-century German folklorist Jacob Grimm wrote of as being, presumably, even blacker than that.

In the Middle Ages, the malevolent variety of elf was routinely accused of causing any sudden sharp pains and nightmares, the former by firing invisible ammunition known as elf-shot, and the latter by sitting heavily on a victim's chest during sleep. The German *Albtraum* (nightmare) literally means "elf-dream." Elves were also suspected of causing hiccups and tangling children's hair into "elf-locks" at night. In England, at least as far back as the tenth century, books of remedies advised sufferers on how to minimize the elves' evil effects.

LIGHT ELVES

The *Prose Edda* may also have been the inspiration for the modern crossover between elves and fairies, as Sturluson mentions a third category of elf: the *Ljósálfar* (light elves). These are pale-colored and more beautiful than the sun, and they live in a blissful paradise called *Álfheimr* (Elf-Home, the inspiration for J. R. R. Tolkien's Elvenhome). This distinction between angelic and subterranean elves matches the *Seelie* (blessed) and *Unseelie* (wicked) courts of Scottish fairy legend (see page 19), the folklore equivalents of heaven and hell.

> IN THE MIDDLE AGES, ELVES WERE SUSPECTED OF CAUSING HICCUPS AND TANGLING CHILDREN'S HAIR INTO "ELF-LOCKS" AT NIGHT.

By the nineteenth century, elves had become so interchangeable with fairies that they more often than not had starring roles in heart-warming fairy tales. Hans Christian Andersen's *The Elf of the Rose* (1839) is the story of a solitary little elf—so little that he is imperceptible to the human eye—who spends his days flying from flower to flower and dancing on the wings of butterflies. His tiny size allows him to witness the terrible betrayal of a beautiful girl by her jealous brother, who chops off the head of the girl's beloved fiancé. The elf enlists the help of his friends: the flowers send forth their intoxicating spirits to poison the brother in his sleep, while the bees ensure that the murdered lover's buried remains—and the truth—are finally uncovered.

CHRISTMAS ELVES

Nowadays the best-known "light elves" are those who work year-round to help Santa Claus make Christmas presents. These cheerful green helpers emerged in the US around the middle of the nineteenth century, although their exact genesis is as murky as the location of the workshop in which they prepare Santa's sleigh. One theory is that we owe Christmas elves to "A Visit from St Nicholas" (1823) by American poet Clement Clarke Moore, which is now better known as *The Night Before Christmas*. This was the basis for the jovial Santa we know today, described in the poem as "chubby and plump, a right jolly old elf." By the middle of the century it was not Santa but his staff who were elves: a 1857 poem published in *Harper's Weekly* explained that he "keeps a great many elves at work…to make a million of pretty things." By the end of the nineteenth century, the elves of the North Pole—or Lapland, or somewhere in Scandinavia—were an integral part of American Christmas folklore.

ELF

A Christmas elf that can't make toys is no use to Santa at all. And so it is that Buddy, a human adopted as an elf when he was a baby, and played by Will Ferrell in the 2003 New Line Cinema film *Elf*, is sent by Santa back to where he really belongs: his hometown of New York City. Here, the green-stockinged elf-man tries to forge a relationship with his birth father, a cynical publisher of children's books who not only wants Buddy out of his life—but also does not believe in Santa.

A MIDSUMMER NIGHT'S DREAM

Fairies show both sides of their nature in William Shakespeare's *A Midsummer Night's Dream* (c.1595), in which Oberon and Titania, king and queen of the fairies, are locked in bitter dispute over custody of a changeling. To spite his wife, Oberon has his servant, the mischievous Puck, give Titania a potion that will make her fall in love with the next creature she sees—which turns out to be Bottom, a rough laborer whom Puck has given the head of an ass. While Titania is distracted by her new beau, Oberon snatches the changeling.

Fairies

The best known of the little people, fairies are usually depicted as beautiful and benevolent, but they have a spiteful, self-serving side too.

F airies are the undisputed queens and kings of the little people. Although they cannot be traced as far back as some of their more mischievous brethren, their benevolence has, over recent centuries, elevated them to a position of great respect; little wonder that stories of fantastical diminutive beings have, since the late seventeenth century, been known simply as "fairy tales."

The traditional image of a fairy is a small, delicate, elegant being that can fly using either gossamer wings or magic. In paintings and stories, fairies are almost invariably female, but their male counterparts, though slightly less entrancing in appearance, do exist. Fairies are kind to humans and kind to nature: they are most likely to be found in woodland clearings and overgrown gardens, flitting from flower to flower with the bees and butterflies. Certain plants, including the hawthorn and foxglove, are so precious to fairies that human meddling can result in pain or poisoning.

The word "fairy" comes from the Latin *fata*, "the Fates"—an apt etymology given that fairies often appear in stories to influence the fate of humans. Among the best-known guiding fairies are the Fairy Godmother from Charles Perrault's *Cinderella* (1697) and the Fairy with Turquoise Hair in Carlo Collodi's *Adventures of Pinocchio* (1883).

THE UNSEELIE COURT

Before fairy tales changed their fortunes for the better, fairies were not always known for their kindness. A traditional Christian interpretation of fairies was that they were fallen angels—not good enough for heaven, not bad enough for hell. They were essentially trapped on Earth.

According to Scottish folklore, fairies are split into two courts: *Seelie* ("blessed") and *Unseelie* ("wicked"). While members of the Seelie Court might be a little mischievous, the Unseelie Court is more malevolently inclined. Wicked fairies often travel in packs, leading travelers astray or even assaulting them.

A dark practice commonly associated with fairies in folklore tales from around the world is the switching of a human child with a fairy child, or "changeling." Such beliefs were particularly prevalent in the Middle Ages, when children were more prone to sudden and inexplicable illness or even death; in the absence of scientific knowledge, it seemed just as likely that the fairies had spirited away the real child and left a defective one in its place.

The German writer Johann Wolfgang von Goethe played on this terrifying theme in his 1782 poem "Der Erlkönig" ("The Fairy King"). A man rides through the night with his child in his arms, but the child sees ever more visions that the father cannot: the Fairy King with his crown and robes; a host of beautiful fairy princesses. In whispered promises the child is lured toward this other world—and is dead by the time the father gets home.

FAIRIES ARE MOST LIKELY TO BE FOUND IN WOODLAND CLEARINGS AND OVERGROWN GARDENS, FLITTING FROM FLOWER TO FLOWER WITH THE BEES AND BUTTERFLIES.

THE COTTINGLEY FAIRIES

In 1917, cousins Elsie Wright, 16, and Frances Griffiths, 9, photographed the fairies at the bottom of their garden in Cottingley, Yorkshire. One showed Frances watching four fairies dancing on top of a hedge, and another was of Elsie playing with a gnome. They told their parents that the creatures could only be "ticed" out when nobody else was watching. The photos came to the attention of Sir Arthur Conan Doyle, creator of Sherlock Holmes. He was convinced that they were genuine, and in 1920 gave the cousins a new camera each to take more photos. Three further pictures emerged, including one of the fairies dancing in their "sun-bath." Doyle was delighted with the results and in 1922 wrote *The Coming of the Fairies*. Toward the end of their lives, the cousins admitted that the photos had been a hoax—the credulity of an intellectual of Doyle's renown had made it impossible to reveal the truth—all except the last one, *Fairies and their Sun-Bath*, which Frances continued to insist was genuine.

THE NOME KING

Hollywood may have pushed him aside to make way for the Wicked Witch of the West, but one of the wickedest baddies in L. Frank Baum's *Oz* novels is the Nome King, also known as Roquat the Red and Ruggedo. First appearing in *Ozma of Oz* (1907), set five years after *The Wonderful Wizard of Oz*, the Nome King presides over a kingdom of underground treasure-hoarders. He is immortal but for one fatal flaw: he is violently allergic to eggs.

Gnomes

These ancient, earth-dwelling treasure-hoarders keep to themselves and are rarely seen...but they'll go to extraordinary lengths to do your gardening.

Gnomes are spirits of the earth, similar in appearance to dwarves but with their own unique characteristics. Like dwarves, they are generally described as short, bearded, benevolent old men, although gnomes are easily distinguishable by their pointed red hats (or green for the females). They live underground, where they are able to walk through the earth as easily as we humans walk through air. It is generally believed that gnomes spend much of their time guarding their vast hoards of treasure, although they will also come to the aid of trapped or injured animals.

These ancient beings were not given the name "gnome" until relatively recently. Writing in the early sixteenth century, Swiss occultist and alchemist Paracelsus identified four classifications of "elementals," creatures that correspond to the four elements of life: nymphs for water, sylphs for air, pygmies (or gnomes) for earth, and salamanders for fire. He chose the term *gnomus* to denote "earth-dweller," and described these little men as being highly averse to human contact.

GARDEN GNOMES

Although gnomes can roam easily underground, their movement is severely restricted when they appear above the surface. Most cruelly, given their fondness for gardening, gnomes turn to stone upon exposure to sunlight. There is a loophole, however: if they transform themselves into toads, they are free to enjoy people's gardens in disguise. To honor this unfortunate affliction, ceramic garden gnomes—first produced in mid-nineteenth-century Germany—have become common sights the world over. By day the gnomes seem to be made of stone, but at night they come to life and spend our sleeping hours tending to plants and animals.

Goblins

These malevolent sprites will go to extreme lengths to get whatever they want, be it food, gold, or human life.

While most other mythical little people counter their unexceptional looks with a noble demeanor or altruistic character, goblins have no saving grace whatsoever. Angry, ugly, and mischievous bordering on willfully wicked, goblins delight in causing chaos wherever they roam—which is far and wide, for they are wanderers by nature. They sleep in caves, holes, or hollow trees, but worst of all can invade family homes, where they pinch and prod the inhabitants, tear furniture to shreds, turn food rotten and milk sour, and frighten people almost (or literally) to death.

EVIL GIFTS

Modern-day goblins are thought to be the descendants of the kobold of pre-Christian Germanic folklore, which in turn can be traced back to the kobaloi of ancient Greece, shape-shifting little thieves who harassed humans at every opportunity and were used in stories to terrify children into obedience.

Christina Rossetti's poem "Goblin Market," published in 1862, harks back to this ancient Greek tradition, although hers is a particularly chilling cautionary tale. Two sisters, Lizzie and Laura, hear goblin merchants offering their wares—"Plump unpeck'd cherries, melons, and raspberries, bloom-down-cheek'd peaches, swart-headed mulberries…" Even though she knows these are "evil gifts," Laura is seduced by the goblins' cries and eats the fruit—only to fall into a terrible sickness. Lizzie has to confront the scratching, pinching, kicking goblins to save her sister, and both live to strike mortal fear into their own children with tales of "the wicked, quaint fruit-merchant men, their fruits like honey to the throat but poison in the blood."

LABYRINTH

As charming as he is sinister, Jareth the Goblin King, played by David Bowie in the 1986 film *Labyrinth*, perfectly embodies the seductive lure of goblins. When Sarah casually invokes the Goblin King to come and take away her baby brother, her wish is granted, and she is forced to navigate his obstacle-strewn kingdom in order to retrieve the child. Finally she remembers the line that will release them both: "You have no power over me!"

GREMLINS

The 1984 film *Gremlins* reinforced the idea that these were creatures not to be messed with. Sweet, fuzzy Gizmo is bought as a pet, but he comes with some serious warnings: he must never be exposed to bright light or water, and never be fed after midnight. When these rules are inevitably broken, Gizmo spawns a host of wicked, razor-toothed gremlins that wreak havoc, destruction, and even murder.

GREMLINS

These mischievous monsters have an appetite for destruction and cannot be house-trained. Under no circumstances are they to be bought as pets.

Gremlins are among the youngest mythical creatures ever discovered: they are approximately as old as the era of aviation, and that is no coincidence. Gremlins just love planes—or, rather, they love destroying planes, and any other machinery they can get their teeth into.

Pilots flying missions in World Wars I and II were the first to identify these interfering monsters, who caused planes to malfunction with creative sabotage methods including messing with controls, ripping out cables, and scrambling radios. Some airmen even claimed to have seen the creatures gleefully tinkering with machinery midair. The name "gremlin" is thought to derive from the Middle English *gremian*, "to provoke or vex."

A WAR ON MACHINERY

By the middle of World War II, gremlins were well-known menaces and, crucially, they seemed to have no interest in taking sides: airmen of all nations were prone to gremlin sabotage.

In 1943, a former Royal Air Force fighter pilot who had fallen prey to gremlins and crash-landed in the North African desert published his first children's book, *The Gremlins*. For once these mean-spirited beasts had wrought some good: Roald Dahl, the fighter pilot in question, went on to become one of the greatest children's authors the world has ever known.

When they tired of planes, gremlins moved into other areas of industry. In the United States, they starred in a series of wartime health and safety posters bearing slogans such as "Gremlins are floor greasers: watch your step!"

Gremlins have adapted well to the modern age and are more versatile than ever before, interfering with everything from traffic lights to Internet connections. Next time your computer crashes without any warning: you'll know what to blame.

HARRY POTTER AND THE
CHAMBER OF SECRETS

In *Harry Potter and the Chamber of Secrets* (1998), the second book in J. K. Rowling's Harry Potter series, the eponymous hero makes the acquaintance of a put-upon creature named Dobby. Although he is described as a "house-elf," Dobby is in many ways the archetypal house sprite: he is an uncomplaining household helper—albeit to the sinister Malfoys—and warns Harry of impending danger. Crucially, it is only when Harry tricks Lucius Malfoy into giving Dobby some clothes that the sprite is freed from his obligation to serve the family.

House Sprites

These little men just want to do your housework in peace. If you try to thank them, they will run away and never come back.

While most little people revel in the freedom of life outdoors, living in tree hollows or beside brooks, there is a class of diminutive sprites who love nothing more than the warmth and shelter of a human home. Usually they remain hidden until night falls, when they can have the house all to themselves. And they repay their unwitting hosts too, by performing their fair share—often more—of all sorts of household tasks.

BROWNIES

It is a happy home that can boast its own brownie, a helpful little sprite of Scottish origin that is defined in sixteenth-century ballads and fairy tales as "a wee brown man." Often brownies live in the barn adjacent to a house rather than in the family home. Although they can sometimes be heard cleaning and polishing at night, brownies are intensely private and do not want to be seen. They are receptive to gifts of milk, cream, honey, and porridge, so long as they look like leftovers; any sort of formal payment is liable to offend the brownie and send him in search of a new residence. A well-meaning gift of clothing is likewise deemed a terrible insult.

In Scandinavia, brownies are known as *nisse*, *tomte*, or *tonttu*. These sprites, which resemble little old men but are incredibly strong, protect farmers and their families and animals, especially at night. They are particularly fond of horses and will go so far as to braid the tail of their favorite horse—but conversely they have been accused of punishing interfering humans by tying the tails of their cows together.

In Russian traditions, homes are protected by a bearded little man called a *domovoi* ("man of the house"). *Domovye* tend to be rather more formal than brownies, requiring a family to don their Sunday best and loudly invite them in, but once safely installed behind the stove they will guard their hosts jealously, forewarn them of danger, and help with household chores.

HOBS AND HOBGOBLINS

In English folklore the hobgoblin began life as a household spirit—the name either means "goblin of the hob" or, in sixteenth-century northern English dialect, "elf-goblin"—but by the seventeenth century had become better known for mischievous pranks. One theory about the word's etymology is that "hob" is a nickname for "Rob," specifically "Robin Goodfellow," a name given to many mythical sprites of the period, most famously the character better known as Puck in Shakespeare's *A Midsummer Night's Dream* (c.1595). Encountering an unknown fairy, Puck's reputation precedes him: "You are that shrewd and knavish sprite call'd Robin Goodfellow: are not you he that frights the maidens of the villagery. . .mislead night-wanderers, laughing at their harm? Those that Hobgoblin call you and sweet Puck, you do their work, and they shall have good luck."

> BROWNIES ARE RECEPTIVE TO GIFTS OF MILK, CREAM, HONEY, AND PORRIDGE, SO LONG AS THEY LOOK LIKE LEFTOVERS; ANY SORT OF FORMAL PAYMENT IS LIABLE TO OFFEND.

HEINZELMÄNNCHEN

In Cologne, Germany, nocturnal housework used to be done by a band of house sprites known as the *Heinzelmännchen*. *Männchen* means "little men," although the name is thought to come from *Heinzelmännlein*, a German word for the mandrake plant, which has hallucinogenic qualities and in many myths can come to life as a small imp-like creature. *Heinzelmännchen* first appeared in an 1826 poem by Ernst Weyden, which reminisces about the "good old days" in Cologne when workers could wile away their days in gluttonous laziness, safe in the knowledge that the *Heinzelmännchen* would do all their work for them at night. They would clean for housewives, bake bread for the baker, hack meat for the butcher, fill wine barrels for the cooper, and cut cloth for the tailor. Until one night, when the curious tailor's wife tried to catch the *Heinzelmännchen*. She scattered dry peas on the floor of the workshop; they slipped and created a terrible racket, but when she appeared with her candle they vanished—and were never seen again. To this day, the people of Cologne atone for their treachery by doing their own work without the help of house sprites.

Leprechauns

Ireland's national mascot has long been hunted for his legendary crock of gold. But the leprechaun just wants to get on with his job.

Leprechauns have become so synonymous with Irish culture that St Patrick's Day—ostensibly marked to commemorate the saint's conversion of pagans to Christianity in the fifth century CE—has, in non-religious settings, become a festive celebration of these green-clad, orange-bearded, gold-hoarding little fellows.

We only ever think of leprechauns as dressed in green, but as recently as the nineteenth century they were described as wearing red. W. B. Yeats elaborated on this outfit in his 1888 work *Fairy and Folk Tales of the Irish Peasantry*, in which he labeled the leprechaun "something of a dandy." He "dresses in a red coat with seven rows of buttons, seven buttons on each row, and wears a cocked-hat, upon whose pointed end he is wont…to spin like a top when the fit seizes him." The sartorial switch to green seems to have occurred in the early twentieth century, alongside an increased commercial association of all things shamrock-green with Ireland.

HARD WORK PAYS OFF

Like other mythical fairy-folk, leprechauns are diminutive; their name in Irish, *leipreachán*, is made up of the Old Irish words for "small" and "body." A conflicting etymology holds that the name comes from *leith bhrogan*, "the one shoe-maker," for leprechauns spend their days industriously fixing shoes for the fairies, who are forever wearing them out through dancing.

Leprechauns are solitary creatures—not least because there are no females of the species—and prefer to keep to themselves, quietly cobbling. But their constant tap-tap-tapping tends to give them away, as evoked by nineteenth-century Irish poet William Allingham in "The Lepracaun": "Tip-tap, rip-rap, tick-a-tack-too! Scarlet leather, sewn together, this will make a shoe."

Humans have good cause to listen out for this tapping; snaring a leprechaun could, as Allingham explains, make you "a made man." Besides cobbling, leprechauns are known for their overflowing crocks of gold, which they hide at the ends of rainbows. How they came to be so wealthy from time-consuming manual labor is unclear, but one theory is that they are merely the trustworthy guardians of other sprites' treasure.

FRIENDS IN HIGH PLACES

For all the light-hearted jollity that surrounds leprechauns, the little men are descended from a surprisingly illustrious line. In the pagan era before St Patrick, Irish mythology was presided over by the brave and powerful *Tuatha Dé Danann* ("Followers of the Goddess Danu"), one of whom, the goddess Ériu (Éire in modern Irish), gave her name to Ireland. As Christianity grew to dominance, these deities were explained away as having retreated to the Otherworld, and were reinterpreted by religious leaders as mythical kings, or fallen angels. Gradually they were absorbed into a broad group of mystical beings known as the *aos sí*, "mound-dwellers," which counts among its number elves, fairies, and leprechauns.

Leprechauns have two very close relatives within the *aos sí*; Clurichauns are ill-tempered, nocturnal creatures, who bear a close resemblance to the leprechaun but are entirely opposite in work ethic. They like nothing more than downing tools and getting blind drunk. Far darrigs, "red men," are rather more rodent-like in appearance, which befits their shrewd and devious brand of cruel practical joke, such as planting nightmares in people's minds, or making ghostly sounds in the dead of night.

> LEPRECHAUNS PREFER TO KEEP TO THEMSELVES, QUIETLY (OR SO THEY THINK) COBBLING. BUT THEIR CONSTANT TAP-TAP-TAPPING TENDS TO GIVE THEM AWAY.

LEPRECHAUN LEGACY

As recently as 1989, an Irish publican named P. J. O'Hare found what he identified as a leprechaun suit on Foy Mountain in Carlingford, County Louth. Beside it was a patch of scorched earth and the remnants of what could only, in the circumstances, be leprechaun bones. In the suit pocket were four gold coins. The incident inspired the annual National Leprechaun Hunt as well as a long, and ultimately successful, campaign to have leprechauns officially declared a protected species by a European Union directive.

DARBY O'GILL AND THE LITTLE PEOPLE

Sean Connery played the romantic interest in Disney's 1959 feel-good film about a man kidnapped by leprechauns. *Darby O'Gill and the Little People*, based on the novels of Herminie Templeton Kavanagh, sees a retired pub regular with the gift of the gab spirited away by Brian, King of the Leprechauns. He is granted three wishes and manages to escape, but has to use his last wish to spare his daughter from the curse of a banshee.

Pixies

Pesky pixies just want to play, but their reckless pursuit of frivolity often puts them at odds with, well, anyone and everyone.

Pixies (or piskies or even pigsies) are a species of fairy-like creatures native to Devon and Cornwall in the South West of England. Like fairies they are small, nimble, and generally full of joy, although they lack the wings and elegance of their fairy comrades. They tend to be red-haired with pointed ears, wearing green rags and pointed hats.

Above all, pixies love to play, and will contrive spurious reasons to put on a colorful carnival or even lure human children to join them in a dizzying dance. They are particularly partial to horse riding, and have been known to steal horses and ride them round and round in wild circles.

Pixies are usually kind to humans, although their relentless form of mindless mischief has occasionally led to clashes.

PETER PAN

In J. M. Barrie's 1904 play *Peter Pan* and his 1911 novel *Peter and Wendy*, Peter's friend Tinker Bell is a fairy. But for the 1953 Walt Disney animated feature film, she was transformed into a winged pixie, whose magical "pixie dust" gives the children the power to fly. Since the 1950s she has frequently been featured in the opening credits of Disney films, sprinkling pixie dust over Sleeping Beauty's castle.

THE PIXIE REVENGE

While pixies are believed to predate Christianity in Britain, their precise origin is unknown, but what is certain is that they are not fond of organized religion. The Devon town of Ottery St Mary, to this day, prides itself on having successfully chased out its pixie nemeses on Midsummer's Eve 1454, following 800 years of anarchic mayhem. When the bells of the parish church rang out for the first time on that day, the pixies fled in terror—only to return and abduct the town's bell-ringers. An annual midsummer festival known as Pixie Day now commemorates the "Pixie Revenge," and the streets of Ottery St Mary are filled with children dressed as pixies, who chase the bell-ringers out of town before welcoming them back with great fanfare.

CHAPTER 2

DEMONS & THE UNDEAD

From bloodsuckers and brain-eaters to restless spirits
and harbingers of death, the beings in this chapter are
the stuff of nightmares—and Hollywood films. Mankind
has always had a grim fascination for what might await
on the other side of death, and these gruesome creatures
are here to show us the very worst of it. Whether they
come to haunt, curse, or devour us whole, the undead
cross uninvited into the living world, dragging all the
horrors of the afterlife with them.

Banshees

In the dead of night, when you least expect it, beware the eerie wail of the banshee, for it heralds an imminent death.

I n Irish folklore, the banshee (*bean sídhe*: "woman of the fairies") appears in people's homes at night and emits a bloodcurdling wail that calls one of the inhabitants to his or her death. She is traditionally associated with Ireland's five great clans—O'Brien, O'Connor, O'Grady, O'Neill, and Kavanagh— for whom, legend has it, she also performs the Irish funeral ritual of keening (wailing in grief) for the dead.

In appearance, the banshee can be either young and beautiful or old and hag-like, wrapped in a gray cloak or funeral shroud. Her long hair—red or gray, depending on her age—is brushed with a silver comb, which has led to a common Irish superstition that finding a comb is an omen of bad luck.

FATE AND FURY

The banshee is often linked with the Morrigan, an Irish fate or goddess who foretells death on the battlefield. Traditionally made up of three sisters in one eerie manifestation, the Morrigan flies above armies in the form of a crow. In Scotland, imminent death is presaged by the *bean nighe* ("washer at the ford"), a gruesome hag who is seen washing blood from the clothes of someone who is soon to die. She too is known for appearing to doomed soldiers on the battlefield. According to legend, King James I of Scotland was visited by a banshee in 1437, just days before his brutal murder at the hands of rivals for the throne.

TRIUMPHS OF TURLOUGH

The earliest written reference to banshees is thought to be in the 1380 text *Cathreim Thoirdhealbhaigh*, or *Triumphs of Turlough*, a history of the O'Brien clan by Seán mac Ruaidhri Mac Craith. An account of the clan's battles with their Anglo-Norman enemies, the book is notable for its earnest report of the military interventions of three mysterious women, one beautiful and the others "loathly," "ulcerated," and "pustulous," who lead unwitting armies of both sides to their doom.

Demons

Once known for their wisdom and guidance, demons have undergone the sort of personality shift that is nowadays ascribed to their victims.

I n classical mythology, demons were spirits that were neither good nor evil. To distinguish them from the malevolent modern definition of the word, their name is usually spelled either *daimon* (Greek) or *daemon* (Latin), both of which simply mean "spirit." The Greek *daimon* was originally perceived as a benevolent guide or muse, an invisible force that would shape a person's character for the better. Over time the term also came to be applied to the supposed supernatural force that influenced a person to act badly, against their will or nature, which is closer to the definition we understand today.

This evil sort of demon became more dominant as the Abrahamic religions—Christianity in particular—overtook classical mythology, having become conflated with the idea of fallen angels. Chief among these is the angel Lucifer ("Light Bearer"), who defied God and was thrown out of heaven, and who was subsequently interpreted as being one and the same as Satan. The idea of Satan's host of demonic, malformed minions has captured popular imagination since the dawn of Christianity. In his epic 1667 work *Paradise Lost* the poet John Milton gave the netherworld kingdom, "the high capital of Satan and his peers," the name "Pandemonium": "All Demons."

DEMONIC POSSESSION

When we think of demons nowadays, we tend to think of demonic possession: the occupation of a person's body by evil, foul-mouthed spirits. Much of this is thanks to the Hollywood film *The Exorcist*, but such fictional representations are based on very real fears, and allegedly real experiences. Typical symptoms of demonic possession include speaking in tongues or in a voice that is not the victim's own, suffering fits, and undergoing a complete change of personality.

Unsurprisingly, given the association of demons with Satan, the Bible gives a

THE EXORCIST

Details of the 1949 "Roland Doe" case are sparse but riveting, and they inspired William Peter Blatty to write a novel based on the case: *The Exorcist* (1971), which Blatty himself adapted into an Oscar-winning film in 1973. In this version, the possessed child is a young girl, Regan, whose behavior quickly goes from strange to diabolical after she plays with a Ouija board. Just like Roland Doe, Regan assaults her exorcists physically and verbally, until one of them is forced to make the ultimate sacrifice in order to save her.

number of examples of apparent demonic possession. In the Book of Mark, Jesus is said to have "cast seven demons" out of Mary Magdalene. In Matthew, he removes the demons from two possessed men and transfers the spirits into some nearby swine, who run wild and throw themselves into the sea.

Stories of demonic possession continued into the modern age, although they reached a peak during the transatlantic witch hysteria of the seventeenth century. In 1671, Elizabeth Knapp, a sixteen-year-old maidservant in Massachusetts, began to behave strangely—so strangely that her employer, a Puritan preacher, kept a detailed journal of her apparent possession. Elizabeth would suffer violent fits, seeming incapable of speech one moment and talking in "a grum, low, yet audible voice" the next, "using all endeavors to make away with herself, and do mischief unto others; striking those that held her; spitting in their faces; and if at any time she had done any harm or frightened them, she would laugh immediately." After three months the preacher admitted defeat and ended his journal. The remainder of Elizabeth's story is unknown.

> TYPICAL SYMPTOMS OF DEMONIC POSSESSION INCLUDE SPEAKING IN TONGUES OR IN A VOICE THAT IS NOT THE VICTIM'S OWN, SUFFERING FITS, AND UNDERGOING A COMPLETE CHANGE OF PERSONALITY.

EXORCISM

Just as Jesus did in the Bible, ministers of all faiths have traditionally been summoned to perform exorcisms upon people possessed by demons. Rituals vary from one religion to the next, and depend on the power of the demon and nature of the possession, but common tactics include praying, reading passages from holy scripture, laying hands upon the victim and commanding the demon to depart, sprinkling holy water, exposing the demon to religious paraphernalia such as crucifixes, and burning incense. In all cases, it is the demon rather than the victim who is targeted: once free of possession, the victim's normal life and faith should resume.

In 1949, the exorcism of a teenage boy made newspaper headlines in the United States. The child, nicknamed Roland Doe to protect his identity, seemed to have acquired an unnerving supernatural influence after trying to contact his deceased aunt using a Ouija board. During repeated exorcism by a series of priests, the boy would spew obscenities in Latin and lash out at those around him, and his bed would shake as if of its own accord.

ghosts

Dead but restless, inspiring terror but seeking peace,
ghosts are the most widely reported supernatural
phenomena in the world.

V isible or invisible, transparent or solid, floating or walking: ghosts come
in many guises, all of them unnerving to behold.

Ghosts are the spirits or souls of the deceased: what remains when
the body has ceased to function. Most reported ghosts are those of
dead humans, and they tend to look like the people they once were—although
more often than not they are recognizably from a different plane of existence:
they may be transparent, or hover above the ground, or bear the marks of a
brutal death. Often ghosts are described as colorless, and if they are not wearing
their "normal" clothes they are generally dressed in white flowing rags. Ghosts
are traditionally supposed to make an eerie wailing noise as they appear and
may gesture or mime rather than speak. They can walk through walls and are
impossible to trap.

Although ghosts have a reputation for being scary—for haunting houses or
wreaking revenge on those who wronged them in life—the origin of the word
"ghost" comes simply from an old Germanic word for "spirit" or "soul"; hence
the Holy Ghost (or Spirit) of the Christian faith, which is heavenly but not
hair-raising.

GHOSTLY GOINGS ON

In many ghost stories, there is a specific reason why a soul has been unable to
find peace in the afterlife and is thus condemned to haunt the place where it
lived or died. There are two types of haunting: the "replay" variety, in which an
often gruesome scene from the past is visible in the place where it occurred;
and the "unfinished business" sort, in which the ghost may need to interact with
living people. This might entail avenging its murder or imparting an important
message. Once the task is complete, the spirit should be at peace.

This notion has long inspired storytellers. One of the earliest fictional spirits is the ghost of Clytemnestra in Aeschylus' *Oresteia* (fifth century BCE), who returns to wreak vengeance on Orestes, her son and murderer. Likewise, other famous literary ghosts appear with a purpose: Hamlet's father to reveal that he was assassinated, Scrooge's ghosts to forewarn him of a bleak future if he does not mend his mean ways.

VISIBLE OR INVISIBLE. TRANSPARENT OR SOLID. FLOATING OR WALKING: GHOSTS COME IN MANY GUISES. ALL OF THEM UNNERVING TO BEHOLD.

The very earliest written references to distressed souls are in death rites designed to prevent them. In ancient Egypt, pharaohs were buried with funerary texts that contained spells to guide them in the afterlife and give them the power of "coming forth by day." A sixteenth-century BCE compilation of such invocations, *The Chapters of Coming-Forth-by-Day*, is now more commonly known as The Book of the Dead. The so-called *Tibetan Book of the Dead* (literally *Liberation in the Intermediate State Through Hearing*), composed in the fourteenth century, offers similar guidance to the recently departed; in Buddhism, a soul not blessed with enlightenment can be doomed to spend eternity as a wandering ghost.

HALLOWEEN

Nowadays, the last day of October is a festival of all things ghoulish, from vampires to witches to zombies, but originally "All Hallows' Eve" marked the start of a three-day period of remembrance for the spirits of the dead. A traditional Christian belief holds that departed souls wander the Earth from the day of their death until the first day of November, All Saints' Day, making Halloween their last night to right wrongs, haunt enemies, and generally run amok before disappearing from the Earth forever. In Mexico this same period is celebrated as the Day of the Dead; among costumed parades and other colorful festivities, it is generally believed that the spirits of dead children will return to visit their families on Halloween, with deceased adults reappearing the following day.

In Buddhist countries, the fifteenth night of the seventh month of the Chinese calendar is celebrated as the Hungry Ghost Festival, when the gates of hell are supposedly opened, releasing hordes of starving ancestors who visit their families for a lavish feast. In many homes a chair is left empty at the dining table, inviting the ghost to sit down and enjoy the meal.

GHOSTBUSTERS

Ghosts are notoriously impossible to catch—
unless you are able to procure the services of the
Ghostbusters. In the 1984 Columbia Pictures film
of the same name, three Manhattan
parapsychologists played by Bill Murray, Dan
Aykroyd, and Harold Ramis develop nuclear-
powered proton rays that neutralize evil spirits
and force them into a trap, which proves
incredibly useful when New York is overrun with
ghosts. The film was nominated for two Oscars,
selected for inclusion in the prestigious United
States National Film Registry, and in 2016
remade with an all-female crew of Ghostbusters.

THE STORY OF PERSEUS

In Greek mythology, Perseus is commanded by King Polydectes to behead Medusa—an impossible task given her ability to turn people to stone. But the gods give him a mirrored shield, a helmet of invisibility, a sickle, and winged sandals, and Perseus enters the Underworld. To avoid petrifaction, he looks at Medusa only via her reflection in his shield. Having slain her, he takes the head to King Polydectes—who is turned to stone the second he looks at it.

Gorgons

Part-woman, part-beast, these terrifying crones are cruel, rapacious, and worst of all immortal—with one infamous exception.

With a name derived from the Greek *gorgos*, "terrible," the aptly named gorgons are three winged, snake-haired sisters with the power to turn anyone who looks upon them into stone. The gorgons, either individually or as a group, are among the oldest beings in Greek mythology: in the *Odyssey*, Homer refers to "that awful monster" who can be summoned up from the Underworld; in the *Iliad*, the Gorgo's head is worn as a "grim and awful emblem" of war.

Two of the gorgons, Stheno ("Forceful") and Euryale ("Far-roaming"), are immortal, but their more famous sister, Medusa ("Protector"), was not. In *Metamorphoses*, the Roman poet Ovid attributes Medusa's hair of live snakes to a curse put upon her by Athena. All three gorgons live in the Underworld with their equally terrible sisters the *Graeae* ("Gray Ones"), three withered old hags with only one eye and one tooth between them.

HARPIES

Like the gorgons, harpies have the appearance of human-animal hybrids: the body of a woman with the wings, tail, and talons of vultures. Harpies can be very beautiful as well as foul smelling and hideously ugly, but they are without exception cruel and intimidating foes. As their name, from the Greek *harpuiai*, "snatchers," suggests, they are particularly well known for stealing food from their enemies. In the story of *Jason and the Argonauts*, King Phineus of Thrace is condemned by Zeus to live on an island inhabited by harpies, who swoop down and either devour or defecate on his food whenever he tries to eat.

hellhounds

If you hear a blood-curdling howl on a deserted nighttime road, run for your life. The hounds of hell are on their way.

T he mythological world is full of terrifying, bloodthirsty beasts, but there is perhaps nothing more unsettling than "man's best friend" gone feral. Accordingly, hellhounds have for centuries been seen as heralds of the end of days—certainly the end of days for whoever is unlucky enough to encounter them.

A commonly feared phenomenon across pre-Christian Europe was the Wild Hunt, an apparition of hunters with their savage hounds. This spectral horde was believed to race with great clamor across the sky whenever catastrophe was imminent—a flood, or plague, or defeat in battle. The portent came to be known by various names, among them the Devil and His Dandy-Dogs in Cornwall, the Wisht Hounds in Devon, *Cŵn Annwn* (Hounds of the Otherworld) in Wales, and in northern England, Gabriel's Hounds. Although Jacob Grimm revived the Wild Hunt legend in an 1835 book on Germanic mythology, it was already well enough known for English poet William Wordsworth to refer to it in a sonnet of 1807: "Overhead are sweeping Gabriel's Hounds, doomed, with their impious lord, the flying hart to chase for ever through aerial grounds."

Hellhounds vary in appearance but are invariably huge, either black or white in color, and often with blood red eyes or ears.

"AN HORRIBLE SHAPED THING"

Land-based hellhounds are no less monstrous than their celestial counterparts. The so-called "black dog" is a ferocious canine phantom that, like the Wild Hunt, is believed to signify impending doom. Many black dogs are centuries old, such as Black Shuck, "an horrible shaped thing" that appeared in the parish church of Bungay, Suffolk, in 1577, "in a great tempest of violent rain, lightning, and thunder," leaving a trail of dead bodies in its wake. In Flanders, Belgium,

THE HOUND OF THE BASKERVILLES

In 1901, Britain was gripped by the story of a black dog so large and ferocious that only one man was qualified to confront it: Detective Sherlock Holmes. In Arthur Conan Doyle's *The Hound of the Baskervilles*, Holmes is summoned to help the Baskerville family, long plagued by a ghostly hound thanks to an ancestor's pact with the devil. Holmes's sidekick Watson hears the dog howling at night, while he himself stalks the moors in pursuit of a clue. When the hound finally reveals itself, Holmes deduces that things are not quite what they seem.

ravenous *Oude Rode Ogen* (Old Red-Eyes) is thought to have made off with countless innocent children since the late seventeenth century. South American folklore, meanwhile, features a host of shape-shifting sorcerers who can transform themselves into violent, red-eyed, livestock-killing hellhounds.

The black dog of Connecticut's Hanging Hills is newer, and different in that he lures his victims into a false sense of security: on first appearance, he is small, silent, and benign. But seeing him for a second time serves as a warning. A third visitation is a sure omen of death. In 1898, geologist W. H. C. Pynchon published an article describing an encounter with the black dog seven years earlier. He had seen the creature once before and became wary, but his colleague, Herbert Marshall, dismissed his fear. Marshall had, after all, seen the dog twice before and survived. Inevitably, just moments after the dog disappeared, Marshall slipped on ice and fell to his death from a cliff.

> THE WILD HUNT, AN APPARITION OF HUNTERS WITH THEIR SAVAGE HOUNDS, RACES WITH GREAT CLAMOR ACROSS THE SKY WHENEVER CATASTROPHE IS IMMINENT.

CERBERUS

Hellhounds traditionally stand guard at the gates of cemeteries, but the most fearsome of them all guards the gates of the Underworld, preventing the dead from escaping. In Greek mythology, Cerberus is a dog with many heads—exactly how many is a matter of some dispute. Most stories give him two or three, although in Hesiod's *Theogony*, a genealogy of the Greek gods, Cerberus is described as "fifty-headed," as well as strong and relentless, and partial to devouring raw human flesh. He is the mutant offspring of Typhon, a snake-headed monster, and the half-snake Echidna, whose other children include the multi-headed Hydra. Fittingly, Cerberus is often depicted in Greek art as having a snake for a tail, as well as numerous snakes growing out of his body.

The twelfth and final task of the Twelve Labors of Hercules was to capture Cerberus—alive—and bring him back to King Eurystheus. By this stage, Hercules had successfully overcome the most terrible creatures in all of Greek mythology—among them the Hydra—and so simply stormed into the Underworld, grabbed Cerberus round the neck, and dragged him back to Eurystheus. The king had to concur that Hercules had done everything asked of him, and the hellhound was released back into the Underworld.

Krampus

You'd better watch out: Santa Claus is coming to town…
and he's fallen in with a bad crowd.

Santa Claus may well know if you've been naughty or nice and reward you accordingly, but his worst punishment tends to be a substandard gift. His wholly unpleasant colleague Krampus, on the other hand, will find you, beat you, throw you into a sack, and drag you to the Underworld.

Ironically, for a figure of the festive season, Krampus is thought to be a product of pre-Christian Alpine folklore. In some stories he is the son of Hel, the Norse goddess of death. His appearance is fitting: he has the face of a devil, with two horns, fangs, a long red tongue, and a pelt of black or brown fur. His feet are cloven hooves and his hands are sharply clawed; his name comes from the Middle German *Krampen*, "claw." He carries birch branches or sometimes even a whip in order to beat children who have misbehaved, and his hands are often chained to symbolize his servitude to his considerably more benevolent superior, St Nicholas.

> IF YOU'VE BEEN NAUGHTY, KRAMPUS WILL FIND YOU, BEAT YOU, THROW YOU INTO A SACK, AND DRAG YOU TO THE UNDERWORLD.

KRAMPUSNACHT

In German-speaking countries, parts of Eastern Europe, and above all in the Netherlands, December 6 marks the start of festive gift giving. It is the feast of St Nicholas, a bearded, red-clad man whose name in Dutch, *Sinterklaas*, was the inspiration for "Santa Claus" as an alternative name for Father Christmas. On the eve of St Nicholas' Day, children leave their shoes outside in the hope that the saint will fill them with small presents. Bad-mannered children can expect to find a sprig of birch twigs instead.

Since at least the seventeenth century, Krampus has been thought of as a companion to St Nicholas—his darker side, dispensing punishment where the

good saint dispenses gifts. Consequently, St Nicholas' Night is also Krampus Night, or *Krampusnacht* in German. On this one night—a sort of festive Halloween—the wicked horned creature is said to roam the streets with his weapons of punishment, seeking out children who deserve a good thrashing. In many German and Austrian villages, he really does stalk the streets, rattling his chains and lashing out at bystanders as part of a costumed *Krampuslauf* (Krampus Run).

UNHAPPY CHRISTMAS

The monstrous Krampus is not the only villain associated with Christmas. Another pagan-inspired nemesis to the badly behaved is Perchta, or Bertha, a supernatural, wizened hag who traditionally oversees spinning. In his 1835 encyclopedia of German mythology, Jacob Grimm records the traditional belief that Perchta appears at the end of each year to check on spinners' work and to sabotage any jobs that she finds unfinished. As demanding as she is malicious, Perchta insists that her annual visit is marked by joyless solemnity. It is a fool who dares eat anything more extravagant than fish and gruel on that day: Perchta will punish his insubordination by "cutting his stomach open, filling it with straw, and closing the wound using a ploughshare for a needle and an iron chain for a thread."

In Iceland, one particularly vile family dominates ill will during the festive season. Its matriarch is Grýla, a hideous ogress—sometimes hoofed and horned—who appears at Christmas to make children have a miserable time. Rounding up as many naughty children as she can fit into her giant sack, she carries them back to her mountain lair, where she eats them—or perhaps shares them with her thirteen sinister sons. The troll-like *Jólasveinarnir*, or Yule Lads, keep children in a permanent state of anxiety in the thirteen nights leading up to Christmas, taking it in turns to leave a gift that is either pleasant or putrid depending on the child's demeanor. Completing the family is the *Jólakötturinn*, or Yule Cat, a pet of monstrous proportions and voracious appetite, who descends from the mountains to terrorize, and then devour, anyone who has been lazy during the year.

KRAMPUS

The family tormented by Krampus in the 2015 Universal Pictures film of the same name have not just been bad: they've completely lost their Christmas spirit. Owing to a family curse, Krampus has had his watchful eye on them—and this year's unfestive bickering has caught his attention. When youngest son Max rips up his letter to Santa in frustration and throws it out of the window, Krampus is summoned forth from his lair to punish the family once again.

Mummies

They were carefully buried thousands of years ago...and will wreak their revenge on anyone who desecrates their resting place.

An ancient Egyptian tomb is opened. The mummy inside is woken from its millennia-long sleep of death. It rises up zombie-like, bandages dragging behind it, and wreaks a terrible revenge on those who dared to disturb it. Or so Hollywood would have us believe. In reality, mummies are dead—very dead, in the case of the Egyptian ones dating back to 3500 BCE. They are simply (and literally) incredibly well preserved, giving them the appearance of fresh corpses beneath their linen wraps.

Mummies take their name from the Arabic *mūmiyā*, "embalmed body," probably related to the Persian *mūm*, "wax." The practice emerged in ancient Egypt out of a concern for the welfare of a soul in the afterlife. Initially mummification occurred naturally through the shallow burial of bodies in arid, dehydrating desert sand, but in the third millennium BCE ritualistic mummification became a common procedure, particularly for the rich and powerful.

The most elaborate preparation, and the one most guaranteed to defy decomposition, began with the removal of the brain using a hook up the nose. All other organs were then extracted—save for the heart, which the deceased would need in the afterlife—and preserved in a drying salt called natron. The inside of the body would be washed out with wine and the corpse was then left to dry in natron for forty days, before being rubbed with perfumed oils and filled with sawdust or rags. Wrapping the body in linen was the final step: beginning from the head, embalmers would wind the sheets around the body, sealing the strips with resin and placing amulets between the layers for good luck. Once wrapped in around twenty layers of linen, the whole body was enclosed in a large canvas sheet and lowered into its coffin.

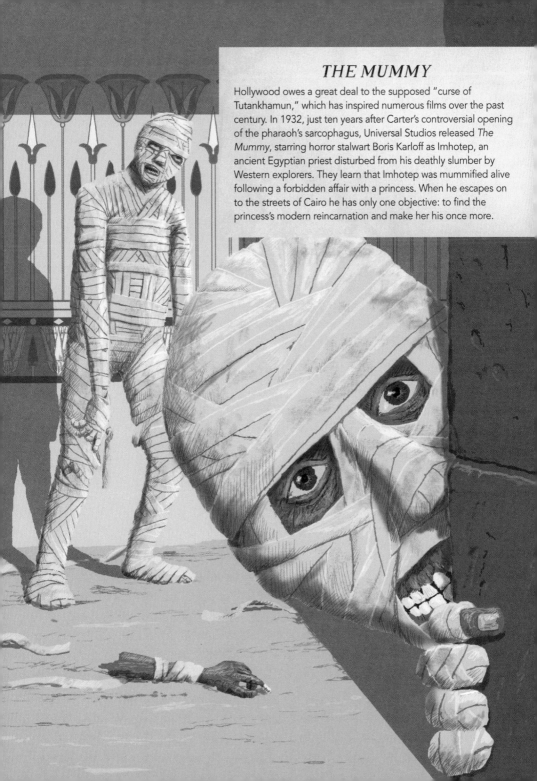

THE MUMMY

Hollywood owes a great deal to the supposed "curse of Tutankhamun," which has inspired numerous films over the past century. In 1932, just ten years after Carter's controversial opening of the pharaoh's sarcophagus, Universal Studios released *The Mummy*, starring horror stalwart Boris Karloff as Imhotep, an ancient Egyptian priest disturbed from his deathly slumber by Western explorers. They learn that Imhotep was mummified alive following a forbidden affair with a princess. When he escapes on to the streets of Cairo he has only one objective: to find the princess's modern reincarnation and make her his once more.

THE CURSE OF THE PHARAOH

When the pharaoh Tutankhamun died at the young age of nineteen in around 1323 BCE, he was mummified according to tradition, with jewels and weapons secreted between the layers of his wrapping, and laid in an ostentatiously ornate burial chamber. Over three millennia later, in 1922, British archaeologist Howard Carter successfully navigated his way to the boy king's long-lost tomb, and lifted the lid of his sarcophagus. Over the course of a lengthy scientific examination, the jewels and other treasures were removed from the mummy, and although the corpse itself remains in its burial chamber in the Valley of the Kings, most of the precious possessions with which Tut was interred are on display in museums around the world.

> BEGINNING FROM THE HEAD, EMBALMERS WOULD WIND LINEN SHEETS AROUND THE BODY, SEALING THE STRIPS WITH RESIN AND PLACING AMULETS BETWEEN THE LAYERS FOR GOOD LUCK.

It was not long after the discovery that rumors began circulating in the Western press about a curse attached to the archaeologists' interference with Tutankhamun's mummy. In early 1923, just weeks after opening the tomb alongside Carter, the expedition's sponsor, Lord Carnarvon, died of blood poisoning; one of his brothers inexplicably died of the same ailment later that year, while the other died at a young age in 1929. A handful of Carter's team expired in unusual circumstances shortly after the discovery, although Carter himself survived until 1939.

ANCIENT REMAINS

Ritual mummification is most strongly associated with Egypt, but accidentally preserved human corpses have been found all over the world—and some of them are considerably older than the pharaohs.

In 1991, a man's naturally mummified remains were found in the Ötztal Alps on the border between Italy and Austria. The man, nicknamed Ötzi, was discovered to be around 5,300 years old; he had bled to death from an arrow wound on his shoulder. Scientists were able to identify his age, birthplace, and final meal from the undisturbed substances in his body.

In 1940, a mummified body wrapped in rushes and animal hide was found in Spirit Cave, Nevada. He was assumed to be an impressive 1,500 years old upon discovery, but a detailed analysis carried out fifty years later revealed him to be 9,400 years old, by far the oldest mummy ever found on the continent.

POLTERGEISTS

Forget white sheets and spooky wails: these malevolent ghostly presences are out to hurt you and harass you until you can take no more.

Poltergeist is a German word meaning "noisy ghost," which almost sounds rather sweet and benign—a mischievous spirit, perhaps. But the name is misleading: poltergeists are noisy, and can be mischievous up to a point, but they are best known for inflicting the most terrifying physical and psychological damage upon the subject of their haunting.

While stories of ghosts have existed for millennia, most stories specifically involving poltergeist activity are much more modern, having come into their own in the nineteenth century. The reasons for this are unclear, although the Victorian-era poltergeist outbreak did coincide with the "Golden Age of the Ghost Story," epitomized by the eerie tales of M. R. James, Edgar Allan Poe, and Charles Dickens. It also coincided with the birth of modern psychological study, followed later in the century by the new field of psychoanalysis. The common nineteenth-century belief among psychologists that women were susceptible to "hysteria" tallied neatly with the fact that females—specifically teenage girls— were seemingly more prone to alleged poltergeist harassment.

PARANORMAL ACTIVITY

Many poltergeist stories support the idea that these spirits haunt a specific person rather than a place, although other residents of the victim's house will likely also witness the frightening manifestations of the poltergeist's tricks. These can include mysterious knocking noises; smashed, lost, or levitating objects; unpleasant odors; items flung by an invisible hand; clothes set on fire; flickering lamps or candles; and, most chilling of all, physical attacks, from pinches and kicks to full-on assault.

While some fantastical creatures only live and operate in a certain country or region, poltergeists are international menaces. One early confrontation occurred in Wiltshire, England, in 1661. Having caused a local drummer to have his drums confiscated, John Mompesson found his house inexplicably filled with the sound of non-stop drumming. The noxious-smelling malevolent spirit would also lift the children out of their beds and move household objects. In 1817, the Bell family of Tennessee came under similar attack: the so-called Bell Witch had an interest in the teenage daughter of the family, who would wake up with welts and slap marks on her body. The trouble only intensified when she became engaged.

In the Bavarian town of Rosenheim in 1967, a law firm was terrorized by an unseen force that would spin paintings on their hooks, fling decorative plates off the wall, cause light bulbs to explode, and move heavy furniture at night. A parapsychologist who came to investigate explained that the lovelorn teenage receptionist had summoned forth telekinetic abilities through her emotional angst.

> **POLTERGEIST TRICKS INCLUDE MYSTERIOUS NOISES; SMASHED, LOST, OR LEVITATING OBJECTS; UNPLEASANT ODORS; CLOTHES SET ON FIRE; AND FLICKERING LAMPS OR CANDLES.**

SPIRITUALISTS AND SÉANCES

Psychologists were not the only group to take a professional interest in the poltergeist mania of the nineteenth century. In 1848, a trio of sisters developed successful careers by communicating with a poltergeist in their home. After hearing strange tapping sounds in the walls of their New York farmhouse, teenage sisters Kate and Maggie Fox convinced their elder sister, Leah, that they had invented a way of "talking" to the spirit of a previous tenant who said he had been murdered and buried in the basement. The sisters began holding wildly popular séances in which the spirit would tap answers to questions—one for "no" and three for "yes."

The Foxes' success inspired a new fashion for séances on both sides of the Atlantic, in which spirits would invisibly rattle the table, touch the participants, and communicate through knocks and noises. The movement surrounding this craze also inspired modern spiritualism—a belief in the possibility of interaction between the living and the dead. Kate and Maggie Fox were among the earliest professional mediums, even though they both later flip-flopped on whether or not their skill was an elaborate hoax. Bones found in their basement in 1904, long after all three sisters had died, did nothing to quell fascination with the poltergeist of what was by then known as "The Old Spook House."

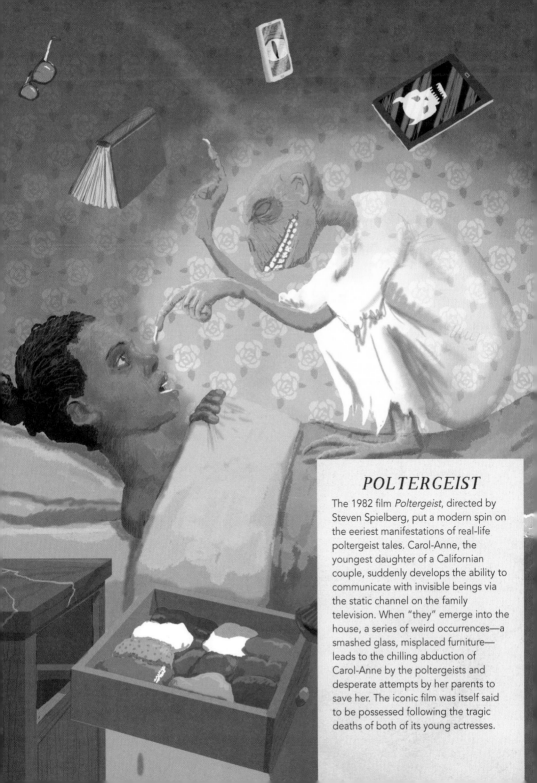

POLTERGEIST

The 1982 film *Poltergeist*, directed by Steven Spielberg, put a modern spin on the eeriest manifestations of real-life poltergeist tales. Carol-Anne, the youngest daughter of a Californian couple, suddenly develops the ability to communicate with invisible beings via the static channel on the family television. When "they" emerge into the house, a series of weird occurrences—a smashed glass, misplaced furniture—leads to the chilling abduction of Carol-Anne by the poltergeists and desperate attempts by her parents to save her. The iconic film was itself said to be possessed following the tragic deaths of both of its young actresses.

Vampires

Rising from their graves at night, vampires stalk the shadows looking for blood. One bite, and you'll be a vampire too.

Y ou're a long time dead, the saying goes; a very long time indeed if you happen to be killed by a vampire. Vampires are the immortal undead— dead but refusing to lie down and die—who prey upon human victims. Emerging from their coffins under cover of darkness, they use their sharp fangs to pierce their victims' necks and then drink their blood. This allows the vampire to "live" another day—and turns the dead victim into a vampire too.

Thanks, in part, to Hollywood films, the modern image of a vampire is a pale-skinned, black-caped man. But the earliest vampire-like creatures were women. In ancient Egypt, the lion-headed goddess Sekhmet was feared for the ease with which she once laid waste to humanity on the orders of the great sun god Ra, acquiring a taste for blood in the process. Lilith, a female demon in Jewish folklore, was considered a particular threat to children, while in Greek mythology Lamia, a wronged lover of the god Zeus, was a ruthless cannibalistic hunter of young blood.

THE TWILIGHT SERIES

Bloodlust is not the only kind of lust with which vampires are associated in literature: from Lord Ruthven to Count Dracula to Edward Cullen, their air of cool mystery makes them intoxicatingly attractive to women. Edward Cullen is the hero of Stephenie Meyer's bestselling Twilight series (2005–08). He may be 104 years old, but he has the appearance of a Hollywood heartthrob (and is aptly portrayed by Robert Pattinson in the film adaptations). Edward's relationship with human teenager Bella Swann is tested by their innate differences—and the attentions of a rival, the werewolf Jacob.

THE REAL-LIFE DRACULA

Hollywood owes its enormously popular vampires to a renewed interest in the blood-sucking creatures in nineteenth-century Europe. An 1819 short story entitled "The Vampyre," by English Romantic writer John William Polidori, is credited with having inspired the vampire mania that followed. In it, a mysterious young nobleman named Lord Ruthven, remarkable for "the deadly hue of his face,

which never gained a warmer tint," goes on a killing spree across Europe before drinking the blood of his own wife on their wedding night.

By the end of the nineteenth century, Gothic horror was so popular that the time was ripe for the greatest vampire story of them all: *Dracula* (1897), by Irish novelist Bram Stoker. Solicitor Jonathan Harker is sent to Transylvania to help a wealthy count, Dracula, arrange his financial affairs before he moves to the windswept English seaside town of Whitby—where it soon emerges that he is a bloodthirsty vampire. All the garlic in Whitby cannot save a young woman named Lucy from becoming Dracula's victim, and subsequently his fellow vampire.

> **THE REAL-LIFE DRACULA WOULD IMPALE HIS ENEMIES ON STAKES—ALIVE— AND LEAVE THEM TO DIE SLOWLY AND PAINFULLY.**

Stoker's novel sounds fantastical but it was inspired by a real-life Transylvanian villain: Vlad the Impaler, a fifteenth-century prince in what is now Romania. The son of Vlad II Dracul, the young prince went by the nickname Dracula, "son of Dracul." Following the assassination of Dracul senior, Dracula fought ruthlessly and successfully to inherit his father's position of power, and then embarked on a reign of terror. His trademark punishment for traitors and foreign enemies was to impale them on stakes—alive—and leave them to die slowly and painfully. The sadistic prince is supposed to have killed tens of thousands of people in this way.

FEARS AND PHOBIAS

Because of their habit of coming back to life, vampires can be incredibly hard to kill. They do, however, have a number of phobias that are relatively easy to exploit. As Bram Stoker knew, garlic is one of them: the pungent plant repels vampires, and nineteenth-century Eastern European legend had it that wearing a garland of garlic would ward the creatures off. To protect deceased relatives from posthumous vampire attack, it was not uncommon for bodies to be buried with a bulb of garlic in their mouths.

Vampires are also repelled by religious paraphernalia, especially crucifixes, and are unable to enter a sacred building. They are also unable to enter a home unless invited—but beware: once in, they can come and go at their leisure. They are defenseless against water, and because they are thought mainly to operate at night, many stories describe vampires withering or melting upon exposure to sunlight. The only sure-fire way to kill a vampire once and for all is to drive a wooden stake through its heart—if you dare get close enough to aim.

ZOMBIES

They've come back from the dead, they can't be killed, and they're ravenously hungry for one thing: your brain!

Z ombies are the undead—or rather the revived dead—but unlike their caped, fanged counterparts the vampires, they lack cunning or charm. All that zombies want is human flesh. Generally lacking emotion, free will, or reason, and exhibiting an advanced state of decomposition, zombies go in search of human prey; once bitten, their victims join the zombie horde. Because they are already dead, zombies are almost indestructible. The only way to defeat them is to target their controlling organ, the brain. According to Hollywood, at least.

The etymology of the word "zombie" is a matter of some dispute, although it is likely to have come from a West African language: the Kikongo *zumbi*, "fetish," or the Kimbundu *nzambi*, "god." In the voodoo religion of Haiti, which is inspired by beliefs brought across the Atlantic by African slaves, a *zombi* is a cadaver brought back from the dead by a *bokor* (sorcerer), who generally then puts the soulless creature to work as a servant.

The Haitian zombie does not eat brains. It most likely resembles the person it was when alive and not under the *bokor's* control. A combination of black magic and potent potions can be used to make a zombie submissive, although powerful *bokor* are thought to have the ability to capture a victim's soul—the *zombi astral*—for use in other rituals and to keep the corporeal part, or *zombi cadaver*, in check.

As recently as 1980, a Haitian man named Clairvius Narcisse claimed to have

SHAUN OF THE DEAD

Night of the Living Dead was such a cult hit that it inspired numerous spin-offs and tributes—including five sequels written and directed by Romero. In 2004, zombie-horror fans Edgar Wright and Simon Pegg released *Shaun of the Dead*, a hit British zombie comedy directed by Wright and starring Pegg as the eponymous Shaun. When London succumbs to a zombie apocalypse, Shaun and his housemate are among the only people not infected, and must fight off the advancing (and ever-reanimating) horde by smashing their brains. Returning the tribute, Romero cast Wright and Pegg as zombies in his fifth zombie film.

been transformed into a zombie. Having ostensibly died and been buried in 1962, Narcisse surprised his family by reappearing eighteen years later. He explained that his brother had paid a *bokor* to poison him into a comatose state that lasted until after his burial. He was then dug up, revived by the *bokor* but drugged into submission, and sent to work at a sugar plantation alongside other zombie slaves. It was only when the zombies managed to murder the *bokor* that Clairvius was able to escape.

A TASTE FOR BRAINS

Credited with introducing zombies—both the concept and the word—to Western sensibilities is William Seabrook, American explorer, author, and occasional cannibal, who traveled to Haiti in the 1920s and published an account of the voodoo rituals he witnessed. *The Magic Island* (1929) captivated readers and was the inspiration for the first of many zombie-related films, including *The White Zombie* (1932), set in Haiti and starring Bela Lugosi as a sinister *bokor* named Murder, who poisons and revives a young woman in a similar way to that described by Clairvius Narcisse.

LACKING EMOTION, FREE WILL, OR REASON, AND EXHIBITING AN ADVANCED STATE OF DECOMPOSITION, ZOMBIES GO IN SEARCH OF HUMAN PREY.

Zombie movies came into their own under the direction of George A. Romero, whose first film, the low-budget *Night of the Living Dead* (1968), is now regarded as a classic of the genre. Set in the US rather than Haiti, the film features the sort of zombies we imagine today: staggering twisted and en masse through residential areas on the hunt for human flesh. Romero went on to write and direct some of the twentieth century's most iconic zombie movies, including *Dawn of the Dead* (1978), although it was not until Dan O'Bannon's *Return of the Living Dead* (1985) that zombies developed a particular taste for brains.

GHOULS

Shape-shifters, grave robbers, and flesh-eaters: ghouls incorporate many of the most terrifying characteristics attributed to Hollywood-style zombies. And they are far more ancient: in Arabic folklore, a *ghūl* is a type of malevolent jinn (see page 170) that is believed to haunt secluded spots, waiting to pick off unwitting travelers. One of the stories in *The Thousand and One Nights* describes them as hideous specters that stalk isolated buildings and graveyards, digging up fresh corpses and feasting greedily on them before reburying the leftovers.

CHAPTER 3

WATER CREATURES

For centuries sailors have reported sightings of strange creatures on the high seas: beautiful mermaids who only want to find true love; heartless Sirens who sing seamen to their watery deaths; and worst of all the Kraken, a gigantic monster that can smash a ship to splinters with one blow. But it's not just the ocean that holds such wild and wonderful beasts: from the bunyips of the Australian billabong and the kappa of Japan to the legendary Loch Ness Monster, it seems no body of water is really safe.

Bunyips

If you go down to the billabong today, you're in for a nasty surprise. And nobody who has seen the bunyip has lived to tell the tale.

I n many ways, the bunyip of Australian folklore sounds like a distant relative of the Loch Ness Monster: this water-dwelling creature of inconsistent appearance lurks quietly beneath the surface until an unsuspecting human is foolish enough to come too close. But as is appropriate for a country with such an impressive list of deadly life forms, the bunyip is a far more chilling prospect than Nessie. For one thing, bunyips come in the plural: there are potentially thousands of them living in creeks, lakes, billabongs, and swamps across the land. The name "bunyip" means "devil" or "evil spirit," and the bunyip is a terrifying creature to behold. Accounts of its appearance vary greatly but common features include dark fur, flippers, and the head of a dog or an emu, with either sharp teeth or tusks.

BUNYIP BONES

Bunyips have been a feature of Aboriginal folklore for thousands of years—exactly how long is unknown because the legend was passed orally from one generation to the next. But when the first European settlers arrived in Australia in the late eighteenth century, they were confronted with tales of this mythical terror—as well as evidence that it might not be quite as fabled as they hoped.

In the first half of the nineteenth century, explorers discovered numerous unidentifiable animal remains in lakes, caves, and beach locations, variously comparing their finds to manatees, walruses, oxen, and elephants. In 1847, the Australian Museum in Sydney even put what it called a bunyip skull on public display, and crowds flocked to see it.

Skeptics believe that such remains must come from a long-extinct Australian mammal—but perhaps, intriguingly, a species unknown to us and witnessed only by early Aborigines.

DOT AND THE KANGAROO

If bunyip terror abated somewhat after the nineteenth century, the 1977 Yoram Gross animated film *Dot and the Kangaroo* resoundingly revived it. This otherwise gentle children's introduction to the wonders of Australian wildlife features a nightmarish sequence about the "bunyip moon," when the fearsome bunyip comes out to feast on human flesh. A fanged monster, "partly animal, partly bird," chases his terrified prey to the ominous strains of a song that warns: "The bunyip's going to get you."

The Hydra

Cut off one head and two more will grow in its place—the Hydra is an adversary worthy of only the greatest hero.

Slaying one dragon is a challenge. Slaying an immortal dragon with an uncountable number of self-regenerating heads should be impossible. And yet, this was a task demanded of the Greek hero Hercules as one of his Twelve Labors. The Hydra that Hercules was sent to slay was a noxious-smelling, many-headed dragon (or more literally a "water snake," from the Greek *hudra*). The fearsome beast was officially known as the Lernaean Hydra, after its lair in the notoriously bottomless swamp of Lerna, famed both for its healing waters and for hiding one of the entrances to the Underworld. The offspring of snake-headed monster Typhon and Echidna, who was half-woman and half-snake, the Hydra counted among its siblings the terrifying multi-headed dog Cerberus, guardian of the gates of the Underworld.

HERCULES' FAILED LABOR

Hercules was the illegitimate son of the great god Zeus and Alcmene, a mere mortal—a transgression for which Hera, the wronged wife of Zeus, vowed to destroy Hercules' life. Thinking ahead, she raised the terrifying Hydra simply to become an unvanquishable adversary for her stepson.

Hercules was dispatched by King Eurystheus, a crony of Hera's, to perform ten impossible "labors," which included slaying, capturing, or hoodwinking the most terrifying monsters in all of Greek mythology. His second task was to slay the Hydra, but it was not a job for one man. His nephew Iolaus accompanied him and, as Hercules chopped off each head, quickly cauterized the stump in order to prevent regeneration.

The Hydra was vanquished but the labor was disqualified when Eurystheus learned Hercules had had help. To punish him for this, and for another task in which he was disqualified on a technicality, Eurystheus added two further tasks, making up the famous Twelve Labors of Hercules.

HYDRA IN THE X-MEN

In the fictional world of Marvel Comics, Hydra is a relentless terrorist organization—enemy of the X-Men—that refuses to be subdued. From the group's first appearance in 1965, Hydra operatives have lived and died according to a motto that harks back to the Lernaean Hydra: if one "limb" is compromised, two more will appear in its place. The organization's one-time leader was Madame Hydra, later Viper, and a long-time adversary of both Captain America and the agents of S.H.I.E.L.D.

LEGENDS OF TONO

In 1912, folklorist Kunio Yanagita published *Tono Monogatari* (*Legends of Tono*), an anthology of local kappa stories he had collected while traveling across Japan. Tales of the mischievous kappa include the creatures' attempts to impregnate human women with their hideous offspring. The city of Tono subsequently became so renowned for its kappa that it is now home to Kappabuchi, a shrine beside a stretch of river in which the kappa is said to live.

Kappa

Hideous water sprite or revered river god, the kappa is a beast that defies description, outwitted only by gifts of courtesy—or cucumber.

The name kappa ("river child" or "river earl") is a catch-all term for dozens of related *yōkai*, or supernatural creatures from Japanese folklore. In the Shinto religion, kappa are considered *suijin*—water deities—rather than monsters, although they tend to display a number of distinctly ungodly characteristics. Found in all inland watery habitats, kappa are generally held to be mischievous if not downright malevolent, and have been associated with a range of crimes, from stealing cattle to violently assaulting humans. Most commonly they are credited with luring young children toward lakes and rivers, then dragging them to their deaths.

Kappa can be appeased by gifts of food, and are particularly partial to cucumber, which in some regions is consumed or thrown into water by people hoping to swim unmolested. The vegetarian sushi roll *kappamaki* is named not for its main ingredient but for the monster/god who would enjoy eating it.

TAKE A BOW

Descriptions of kappa are among the most inconsistent across all fantastical beasts. Their association with water means that scales and flippers, or webbed feet, commonly feature, as does a beak-like snout, much like a turtle's. Other physical attributes might include a shell, a monk-like tonsure, and skin that changes at will from yellow to green. They are the size of a young boy and they smell horribly of fish. The most intriguing feature of the kappa is the concave depression on top of its head. This cavity holds a watery fluid that is the source of the creature's strength; allowing it to evaporate can be fatal. Legend has it that, if cornered, one can thwart a kappa by bowing deeply, as a gesture of reverence. The kappa will be obliged to return the compliment, thus spilling its power and becoming helpless until refilled.

The Kraken

Whether it is a squid, a whale, or a crab is irrelevant. The Kraken is a sea monster of such might and magnitude that no ship is safe in its midst.

The terrifying Kraken is the stuff of sailors' nightmares: a whale-sized squid with tentacles that can snap a ship's mast in two before dragging both vessel and crew to the bottom of the ocean.

It is traditionally supposed to live in Scandinavian waters, and has done so for many centuries. The earliest existing reference to the Kraken is the thirteenth-century Icelandic *Örvar-Odds Saga*, in which the hero encounters "the largest sea monster" in the world, one that is as massive as an island and capable of swallowing whales whole.

SUCH A SWELL AND WHIRLPOOL

Medieval accounts of the Kraken were so believable that, even at the turn of the nineteenth century, a Scottish encyclopedia cited its existence as fact. Paraphrasing *Natural History of Norway*, a comprehensive tome written in 1752 by Bishop Pontoppidan of Bergen, the encyclopedia explains that the Kraken—here "crab-like" rather than a squid—is so enormous that it is impossible to see the whole thing in its entirety. Eyewitness evidence collected by the bishop describes it emerging from the waves and then slowly sinking down, "which is thought as dangerous as its rising, as it causes such a swell and whirlpool as draws everything down with it."

By the time Herman Melville published *Moby-Dick* in 1851, there was a little more skepticism surrounding the Kraken. The *Pequod* encounters a giant squid with long arms like a nest of twisting anacondas, leading Captain Ishmael to wonder whether it might not be one and the same as "the great Kraken of Bishop Pontoppidan"—were it not for "the incredible bulk he assigns it."

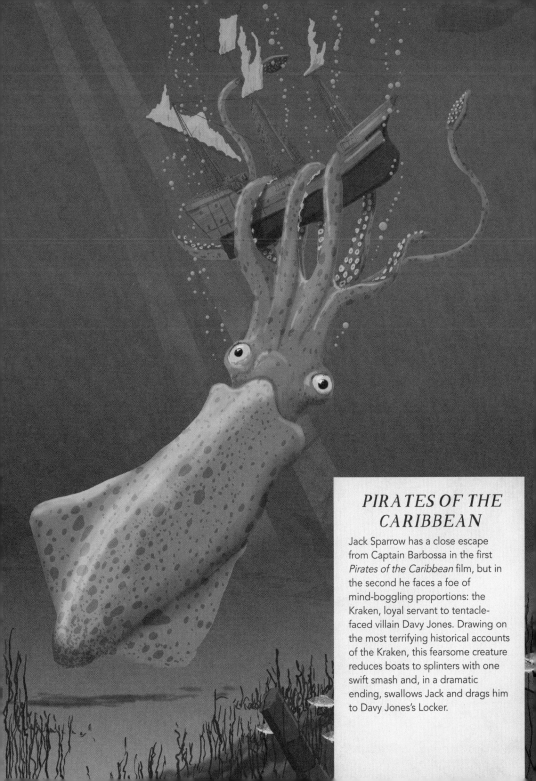

PIRATES OF THE CARIBBEAN

Jack Sparrow has a close escape from Captain Barbossa in the first *Pirates of the Caribbean* film, but in the second he faces a foe of mind-boggling proportions: the Kraken, loyal servant to tentacle-faced villain Davy Jones. Drawing on the most terrifying historical accounts of the Kraken, this fearsome creature reduces boats to splinters with one swift smash and, in a dramatic ending, swallows Jack and drags him to Davy Jones's Locker.

The Loch Ness Monster

Lurking in the depths of one of Scotland's largest lakes is an ancient beast that has often been seen but never yet been captured.

I s it a dragon? Is it a dinosaur? Is it an enormous serpent? Hunters for the Loch Ness Monster—or "Nessie," as it is affectionately known—cannot agree. But one thing is for certain: Nessie is very, very old.

The first Nessie hunter was St Columba, an Irish monk of the sixth century: one of the miracles that eventually earned him sainthood was his defeat of a savage "water beast" in Loch Ness, a vast, deep, and murky lake in the Scottish Highlands. Having heard from locals about the monster's ferocious reputation, Columba made one of his own disciples swim across the loch until Nessie attacked, at which point the monk invoked God and commanded the creature to disappear. A written account of this battle describes the monster as having "a great roar" that inspired "very great terror" in all who heard it.

NESSIE MANIA

St Columba's banishment was certainly effective: the Loch Ness Monster seems to have remained dormant for over a thousand years thereafter. It was not until the nineteenth century that visitors to the loch began reporting strange sightings once more: an enormous splashing beast of indeterminate gender, which variously resembled a giant salamander, a giant eel with a horse's mane, and even an upturned boat. A humped back, or a number of humps, was commonly spotted, and almost every sighting mentioned the creature's impressive speed in the water.

ST COLUMBA SAW A MONSTER WITH "A GREAT ROAR" THAT INSPIRED "VERY GREAT TERROR" IN ALL WHO HEARD IT.

THE WATER HORSE

Nessie has inspired numerous films and television shows, including an episode of *Doctor Who* in which the creature is revealed to be a dangerous cyborg controlled by aliens. A 2007 film adaptation of Dick King-Smith's story *The Water Horse* popularized an intriguing theory about the monster's solitary life and longevity. A young boy living on the shores of Loch Ness discovers a large egg that hatches into a "water horse," described as a genderless creature that, before death, lays a single egg, which itself becomes a solitary Loch Ness Monster—and so the dynasty continues through the ages.

THE SCOTTISH KELPIE

Unlike the solitary Loch Ness Monster, kelpies are a numerous breed and are said to lurk by all of Scotland's lochs and rivers, waiting to lure unsuspecting travelers to their deaths in the water. But this doesn't prevent Scots from being proud to play host to these terrifying beasts. In Falkirk, at the mouth of the Forth and Clyde Canal that crosses central Scotland, two enormous steel kelpie heads were unveiled in 2014. These majestic sculptures, the work of Andy Scott, stand almost 100 feet tall and weigh 330 tons each.

The elusive monster achieved modern fame in the early 1930s, following the construction of a road along the loch's western shore. A spate of sightings by motorists in the summer of 1933 led to a period of intense Nessie mania and a fascination with the creature that continues to this day.

Over the course of the twentieth century, descriptions of Nessie's appearance narrowed into a fairly consistent outline: large, grayish-green, and smooth-skinned, it has a long neck and small head, and propels itself through the water using four flippers and a long tail. The description is so similar to the prehistoric plesiosaur, a marine reptile that roamed the world's oceans between about 200 million and 70 million years ago, that some experts have declared Nessie to be the last survivor of an otherwise long-extinct species.

HORSE MONSTERS OF THE DEEP

Horses feature prominently in descriptions of the Loch Ness Monster. It is often described as having the neck of a horse or the mane of a horse, or a hump that is approximately the size of a horse. The comparison is apt, for Nessie has often been linked with a creature of folklore known as a water horse. Water horses are closely associated with the ancient *hippocampus* (literally "horse sea-monster": half horse, half fish) and the Scottish kelpie, a shape-shifting horse-demon that lives beside lochs and carries weary travelers to their watery deaths. Stories of kelpies were traditionally told in Scotland to stop children from playing near water; in some kelpie stories, the creature can even extend its length to seat a number of victims at once.

CAUGHT ON CAMERA

In 1962, British politicians Sir Peter Scott and David James founded the Loch Ness Phenomena Investigation Bureau, which recruited volunteers to observe Nessie's movements and if possible capture them on camera. After ten long years, researchers managed to take close-ups of what look like Nessie's flippers. Some analysts insist that the images prove the existence of at least two Loch Ness Monsters.

There is definitely a Nessie of sorts lurking beneath the waves of the loch: the long-necked creature photographed in grainy black and white in 1934. To this day, this is the most iconic image of the monster, even though it transpired, after decades of scientific debate, to be a photograph of a plastic submarine with a putty neck and head. The pranksters later admitted that their effigy sank to the bottom of the loch once the photo shoot was over. Nessie hunters are not easily sidetracked by such hoaxes, however, and the search goes on.

Mermaids

**All mermaids want is a chance at love in the human world.
But the biggest wishes come at the highest price.**

Stories of mermaids have existed for as long as mankind has traveled by sea. Sightings by sailors journeying to exotic lands date back to at least ancient Greece, but even Christopher Columbus recorded spotting a trio of mermaids off the coast of the Dominican Republic in January 1493. "They rose high out of the sea," he wrote in his journal, "but they are not at all as beautiful as they are said to be." Little wonder if, as is now commonly supposed, Columbus was looking at a pack of manatees.

The earliest existing mermaid myth is from around 1000 BCE, and tells of the Assyrian goddess Atargatis, who resolved to live as a fish after accidentally killing her mortal lover. She flung herself into the ocean but was too beautiful to become something so ordinary, so she transformed instead into a mermaid ("sea maiden"): a creature with a human head and torso and the tail of a fish.

Mermaids crop up in *The Thousand and One Nights*, a collection of Middle Eastern stories first published in 1717 but thought to date back to the ninth century; in "The Adventures of Bulukiya," the eponymous hero must navigate strange lands inhabited by mermaids, jinn, and other fantastical beasts in order to find the herb of eternal life. While mermaids are usually benevolent creatures, they are closely related to the singing Sirens of Greek mythology, who famously tried to lure Odysseus and his crew to their deaths.

LIFE AND LOVE

Aside from the obvious physical differences, mermaids are remarkably human in both habit and habitat. They enjoy grooming their long, lustrous hair, admiring themselves in mirrors, sitting on rocks and staring out to sea, and singing sweet songs of love. Unlike other sea-dwelling creatures, mermaids live in magnificent underwater palaces adorned with riches.

Nevertheless, it is a lonely existence, and in most folk stories the mermaid

SPLASH

In *Splash*, loosely based on Hans Christian Andersen's fairy tale, a mermaid whose name is a high-pitched squeal sound, played by Daryl Hannah, saves Allen (Tom Hanks) from drowning. She follows him to New York, benefiting from a tail that turns into legs when dry, and love blossoms. But an evil scientist exposes her secret by spraying her with water, and she is taken to a government laboratory for medical testing. Finally able to come to terms with his lover's unconventional background, Allen rescues her and together they leap into the ocean, where he can live forever by her side.

contrives to go ashore in the guise of a human woman in order to find a human husband. Often this means entering into a dubious bargain: human legs in return for mortality, or the loss of her beautiful voice, or beloved mirror and comb. In tales involving such pacts, the mermaid need only retrieve her belongings or contravene the terms of the agreement in order to be cast back into the ocean forever.

OTHER FISH IN THE SEA

There is a very good reason why mermaids need to come ashore to locate a passable husband. Mermen are hideous. Green, bearded, and barnacled, with terrible teeth and seaweed for hair, mermen possess a temper ugly enough to match their appearance, and will conjure up a storm or sink a passing ship for want of anything better to do.

CHRISTOPHER COLUMBUS SPOTTED A TRIO OF MERMAIDS OFF THE COAST OF THE DOMINICAN REPUBLIC. HE WROTE: "THEY ARE NOT AT ALL AS BEAUTIFUL AS THEY ARE SAID TO BE."

The merman Triton is, by a long way, the only credit to his kind. Raised in a golden palace at the bottom of the ocean by Poseidon and Amphitrite, Greek god and goddess of the sea, Triton carries a trident and a conch shell, upon which he blows to announce the arrival of his illustrious father or, more importantly, to calm rough seas.

THE REAL LITTLE MERMAID

Thanks to Disney's 1989 animated feature film, Hans Christian Andersen's Little Mermaid is now better known as Ariel, but in his rather darker 1837 story, ostensibly written for children, she had no name. After saving a handsome prince from a shipwreck, the mermaid falls desperately in love. In her determination to go ashore, she accepts a potion from an evil merwitch—but there are three conditions: the merwitch will take the mermaid's beautiful voice by cutting off her tongue; she will cause every step the mermaid takes upon her human legs to be excruciatingly painful; and if the mermaid fails to ensnare the prince, she will die. Although the prince comes to love the mermaid as a sister, he marries the human princess who he thinks is his savior. The merwitch gives the mermaid one last chance: kill the prince and save herself. But the mermaid cannot bear it. She plunges back into the ocean and turns into sea spray.

SIRENS

**Their hauntingly beautiful voices will lure you to the
water…where their sharp talons will tear you apart.**

I
n Greek mythology, the Sirens are beautiful maidens with human heads
but the bodies, wings, and legs of birds, whose enchanted singing lures
sailors to their doom upon the rocks surrounding their island home. Once
shipwrecked, the unfortunate crew are picked apart and devoured by these
ruthless bird-women.

The Sirens are either the children of Achelous, a river god, or Phorcys, a sea
god. Their mother is said to be one of the nine Muses—either Terpsichore, the
muse of dance, or Melpomene, the muse of singing and tragedy. Their number
is also disputed: in *The Odyssey*, Homer claims that there are two of them;
Hesiod writes of three; other writers claim four. Their habitat is either in or near
the sea, or (according to Homer) "in a flowery field…with corpses all around
them, the flesh rotting away." Many attempts have been made by academics to
locate the Sirens' island. Homer placed it between Aeaea, a mythological island,
and the treacherous rock of Scylla on the southern tip of Italy. An archipelago
near the coast of Capri has so often been identified as the home of the Sirens
that it is known as "the Sirenuse."

SIREN SONGS

Encounters with the Sirens are fraught with danger: their song is so intoxicating
that sailors are powerless to pass them by, and instead are compelled to throw
themselves into the waves. Outwitting the Sirens takes cunning and forethought:
qualities fortunately possessed by the Greek heroes Orpheus and Odysseus.

The Argonautica, a poem composed in the third century BCE by Apollonius
Rhodius, recounts the voyage of Jason and the Argonauts to find the Golden
Fleece. Forewarned that there is no chance of surviving the Sirens without
Orpheus on board, Jason wisely takes the musician with him. When the *Argo*
approaches the Sirens and the first strains of their song is heard, Orpheus takes

up his lyre and plays louder and more bewitchingly than their singing, drowning out the sound of certain death.

Odysseus does not have a lyre to hand in Homer's *Odyssey*, but he does have wax with which to block his men's ears. He, however, is curious to hear the Sirens' song, and so orders his men to lash him to the mast of their ship, to prevent him from leaping into the ocean. "If I beg you to unleash me," he tells them, "tie me tighter still." When he hears the Sirens' fateful song, Odysseus implores his crew to set him free and struggles to loosen the ropes that bind him, but they stick to his orders and sail by in safety.

> ENCOUNTERS WITH THE SIRENS ARE FRAUGHT WITH DANGER: THEIR SONG IS SO INTOXICATING THAT SAILORS ARE POWERLESS TO PASS THEM BY.

RUSALKI AND LORELEI

Sweet-voiced women who lure sailors to their deaths exist in many mythologies. The Slavic *rusalki* are said to be the souls of drowned virgins or unbaptized children, and they haunt lakes and rivers awaiting unsuspecting men that they can ambush and entice into the water. In Eastern Europe, around the River Danube, *rusalki* are thought to be ravishingly beautiful, with long red locks and flowing robes made of mist. Once they get their victim into the water, they use their hair to tie his feet together and drag him down to the depths. In northern Russia, the *rusalki* are hags: hideous old crones who exist only to torture men.

"DIE LORELEI"

The German poet Heinrich Heine developed Clemens Brentano's Lorelei tale in his famous 1824 poem "Die Lorelei," turning a little-known story into a popular legend. The poem reimagines the tragic maiden as a Siren who sits on the rock—the name of which to this day is Lorelei—and enchants sailors with her beauty and her voice. Numerous composers including Franz Liszt have set the piece to music. And it may not be a myth after all: in 2011, an enormous tanker capsized beneath the watchful gaze of a Lorelei statue at the foot of the rock.

On the River Rhine in Germany, a tall rock that produces an eerie echo across the water inspired Clemens Brentano to compose the myth of Lorelei in 1801. A beautiful young woman, Lorelei, is betrayed by her lover and accused of having the power to bewitch men. She is sent away by the local bishop to live in a convent, and on her way there she climbs a tall rock overlooking the Rhine. Thinking that she sees her treacherous beloved down below, Lorelei throws herself into the water, leaving an echo of her name bouncing forever off the cliff.

CHAPTER 4

HYBRID BEASTS

With body parts resembling those of two or more other creatures, the beasts in this chapter are a varied bunch with one thing in common—they are all made up of nature's noblest, mightiest, fiercest specimens. They have lions' heads, elephants' hooves, eagles' wings, scorpions' tails...not to mention their talents for archery or fire breathing. Among human-animal hybrids, most are all the greater for their human intelligence, but to the ancient Greeks there was nothing more monstrous than the Minotaur—half-man, half-bull, a shameful reminder of his unnatural birth.

Centaurs

Noble in appearance but ferocious in demeanor, centaurs rampaged through the ancient world, leaving mayhem and destruction in their wake.

A centaur is a creature from Greek and Roman mythology that has the head, chest, and arms of a man and the body and legs of a horse. Although fantastical in appearance, the notion of a centaur most likely has a very commonplace origin: it arose in Bronze Age Greece following the first encounters between warriors on horseback and cultures without a tradition of horse riding. In Greek mythology, centaurs were thought to live in great herds on Mount Pelion in the region of Thessaly, from which they get their name: *kentauros* was a term applied to a tribe of expert Thessalonian horsemen.

Contrary to modern portrayals in films and literature, centaurs of the ancient world were brutal and destructive; they feasted on raw flesh and were given to drunken rampages, wreaking violent revenge on anyone who stood in their way. In Homer's *Odyssey*, Ulysses is told of the drunken misdeeds of the centaur Eurytion, credited as the origin of the discord between centaurs and humans.

CHIRON

Zeus often used wild centaurs as henchmen, but Zeus also had a brother who was a centaur: the immortal Chiron, unique among his kind as a wise and gentle teacher. In many depictions of Chiron in Greek art, his forelegs are human rather than equine; in some images he even wears robes. As a teacher, Chiron was entrusted with educating Greece's greatest heroes.

THE SILVER CHAIR

The modern perception of centaurs as noble beasts is largely due to C. S. Lewis's Chiron-inspired depiction of them in his Chronicles of Narnia. Throughout the series they are wise, brave, and honest creatures, skilled warriors and defenders of Aslan. Although it is a grave insult for a human to suggest riding a centaur, in *The Silver Chair* a centaur offers Eustace and Jill the great honor of a ride on his back as they travel across Narnia to find a captured prince.

Dragons

They can be the most terrifying of all fantastic beasts,
spitting fire and even poison, or gentle creatures known
for their wisdom and nobility.

With their huge size, scaly green skin, leather wings, razor-sharp teeth, barbed tail, and claws—not to mention the ability to breathe fire—dragons are the ultimate monsters. Although they are predominantly land-based, dragons emerged in Middle Eastern and European folklore as giant serpents; the Greek *drakon* means either "serpent," "water snake," or "giant sea-fish." The dragon's lizard-like body and crocodile scales hark back to this watery origin.

The Mesoamerican creator-god Quetzalcoatl, dating back to at least the first century BCE, was a flying, feathered serpent. He was immensely powerful but generally used his powers for good. The ancient Egyptian serpent-deity Apep, on the other hand, was the long-time nemesis of the sun god, Ra. In Greek mythology, the terrifying monster Typhon, father of the multi-headed serpent Hydra, had a hundred dragons' heads growing out of his gigantic hands. Hercules, as one of his Twelve Labors, had to slay the dragon Ladon, guardian of the golden apples in the Garden of the Hesperides.

Guarding treasure is a common pastime of dragons, and they need to use all of their fearsome physical attributes to ward off the foolish humans who try to steal it. In Norse mythology, the dragon Fafnir poisons anyone who approaches his treasure-filled lair. In the epic Anglo-Saxon poem *Beowulf*, written in around the tenth century, a fire-breathing dragon wages war against Beowulf and his kingdom after a servant steals a golden cup from its stash. This jealous "worm" (serpent) was the inspiration for J. R. R. Tolkien's Smaug, the dragon who sleeps upon an enormous pile of pilfered treasure in *The Hobbit* (1937).

RITUALS AND RELIGION

Chinese dragons are altogether more benevolent than their angry European

PETE'S DRAGON

A winged, green fire-breathing dragon becomes an orphan's unlikely best friend in the 1977 Disney film *Pete's Dragon*. The enormous beast, Elliott, looks fierce but is loyal and lovable—except for his frustrating habit of playing the fool while invisible, leaving Pete to take the blame. The itinerant duo find themselves in a village that is in thrall to a pair of charlatans peddling miracle medicines. When they spot Elliott, the fraudsters determine to capture him and turn him into a money-spinning medicinal product—but catching an invisible fire-breather is not as simple as they hope.

counterparts, and the two beasts seem to have developed entirely independently of one another. They too walk on four clawed feet and have a scaly, snake-like body, but they also have horns and tend not to have wings. In Chinese philosophy, the *lung* (dragon) traditionally represents the yang to the tiger's yin: yang is strong, heavenly, and masculine while yin is passive, earthly, and feminine. Emperors commonly incorporated the powerful dragon into their insignia, and until 1911 it was the main component of the Chinese flag.

> DRAGONS ARE OFTEN THE GUARDIANS OF A GREAT HOARD OF TREASURE, AND NEED TO USE ALL OF THEIR FEARSOME PHYSICAL ATTRIBUTES TO WARD OFF THE FOOLISH HUMANS WHO TRY TO STEAL IT.

Dragons were believed to have power over fertility and rainfall; as early as the sixth century BCE, dragon effigies were used in rituals designed to encourage rain. Colorful dragon dances involving many performers continue to this day, notably to celebrate Chinese New Year.

The *tatsu* or *ryū* of Japan are based on Chinese dragons, and resemble them in most respects; they too control water, including rivers, and have power over the weather. They are strongly associated with Buddhism, and many temples have a shrine to the dragon that is said to live in the nearest lake or pond.

ST GEORGE AND THE DRAGON

A Turkish dragon-slayer makes a curious choice of patron saint for England, but St George has, since the fourteenth century, been the English national symbol of strength and knightly valor. The specifics of the story vary, but legend has it that a terrible dragon had made its home in a spring in Cappadocia, in modern-day Turkey. Since the spring was the only source of water for the local townspeople, they needed to appease the dragon in order to have access to it. At first they managed to keep it happy with a regular supply of sheep to eat, but when the sheep ran out they had no choice but to start feeding the dragon their own children. At last it was the turn of the king's daughter, and although the king pleaded with his subjects to spare her, they all agreed that it was only fair for him to share in their misery. But as the princess stood by the spring waiting for the dragon to emerge, St George appeared on his horse. He made the sign of the cross and charged at the beast with his lance. He then led the wounded dragon back to the townspeople and offered to kill it if all of them—including their king—converted to Christianity, which they gratefully did.

GRIFFINS

Half-lion, half-eagle, the griffin is a magnificent
and mighty beast, and the steadfast guardian of gods,
kings, and treasure.

With the golden-furred body of a lion—the king of the beasts—
and the proud head, wings, and talons of an eagle—the king of
the birds—the griffin is the most majestic of all mythological
creatures. Its name comes from the Greek *gryps*, "hook-nosed," in
reference to its sharp beak.

The myth of the griffin is thought to have originated in Central Asia in the
third millennium BCE, according to one theory, as a result of the
misidentification of dinosaur remains. Its impressive physical might made it a
popular motif in Egyptian artworks depicting gods and pharaohs, and as a sacred
symbol of power and royalty it soon spread westwards to ancient Greece. At the
Palace of Knossos in Crete—home to King Minos in Greek mythology, as well
as the labyrinth that housed the Minotaur—the throne room features a
ceremonial seat flanked on either side by large murals of wingless but regal-
looking griffins with resplendent crests of curls.

GRIFFINS IN THE WILD

The Greek historian Herodotus, writing in the fifth century BCE, recounts the
journeys of a certain Aristeas two centuries earlier, who claimed to have traveled
north, beyond the known Greek world, and encountered a one-eyed tribe who
were locked in a perpetual struggle against enormously wealthy griffins. The
tribe, called the Arimaspians, was forever trying to steal gold from the griffins,
who defended their treasure jealously. The futility of this one-sided battle
between mortals and mighty griffins inspired John Milton, in his epic 1667
poem *Paradise Lost*, to describe Satan's tenacious assault on God's brand-new
Earth as matching the eagerness of a griffin as he "pursues the Arimaspian, who
by stealth had from his wakeful custody purloined the guarded gold."

HOUSE OF GRYFFINDOR

The griffin's powerful features made it a popular heraldic symbol in the Middle Ages, and it is fitting that J. K. Rowling chose Gryffindor as the name of the noblest house at Harry Potter's school, Hogwarts. Although its emblem shows only a lion, the qualities of strength, courage, and vigilance that the griffin embodies are those espoused by the house and its founder, Godric Gryffindor. Hogwarts also boasts its own hippogriffs, chief among them Buckbeak, a fiercely loyal beast who protects Harry from his enemies throughout the series.

According to legend and numerous imaginative artworks of the Middle Ages, the fourth-century BCE Greek conquering hero Alexander the Great devised a flying machine powered by two griffins he had captured on his travels in Asia. He chained the wild beasts to his throne, starved them into submission, and then dangled a piece of meat just out of their reach. In their efforts to get to the food, the griffins ascended into the air, and carried Alexander on a lengthy flight.

FEATHERED FRIENDS AND FIENDS

The griffin may rule the skies but he is not alone up there. In Virgil's *Eclogues* of the first century BCE, the Roman poet used the unlikely coupling of a griffin and a horse as an example of something utterly preposterous—but it was not preposterous to Italian poet Ludovico Ariosto, who in his 1516 poem "Orlando Furioso" developed Virgil's idea into what he called a "hippogriff" ("horse-griffin"). This creature has the wings, beak, talons, and crest of a griffin, with the body and hind legs of a horse. Wild in its natural habitat, the beast can be tamed and saddled for flight.

The large and beautiful *simurgh* of Persian mythology, whose name means "thirty birds," has the head of a dog, the body of a lion, and the wings and tail of a peacock. It is impressively strong, very wise, and very ancient; some legends claim that the *simurgh* is consumed by flames and reborn, phoenix-like, every 1,700 years. Over its long lifetime it has witnessed the destruction of the Earth three times.

> A HYBRID OF THE KING OF THE BEASTS AND THE KING OF THE BIRDS, THE GRIFFIN IS THE MOST MAJESTIC OF ALL MYTHOLOGICAL CREATURES

The Arabian *roc* differs in that it is not a hybrid creature—but it is just as fearsomely enormous as its comrades. This bird of prey resembles a colossal eagle or a vulture, and has an insatiable hunger for all kinds of flesh. The Italian explorer Marco Polo heard of the creature's reputation during a voyage to Africa in the late thirteenth century; he wrote of an eagle large enough to "grab an elephant in its talons and carry it high into the air and then drop it so that it is broken into pieces." Sinbad the Sailor, hero of *The Thousand and One Nights*, encounters a number of *rocs* on his voyages; in one story his boat is smashed apart by boulders dropped upon it by two *rocs*, in retaliation for Sinbad and his crew having feasted on their gigantic chick.

The Minotaur

Half-prince, half-beast, and locked away forever, the Minotaur was the ultimate act of vengeance upon a king who dared deceive the gods.

The Minotaur is as famous for his fearsome appearance—a man's body and the head of a bull—as for his maze of a prison: the inescapable Labyrinth built especially to keep him out of sight. His father, King Minos of Crete, forced this banishment upon him, but it was Minos who had brought the shame of this unnatural offspring upon himself, by incurring the wrath of Poseidon. As punishment for reneging on a promise, the god of the sea made Minos's wife, Queen Pasiphaë, fall in love with a bull. The liaison led to the birth of the Minotaur, or "Bull of Minos," the name adding insult to injury for the cuckolded king.

THESEUS AND THE LABYRINTH

King Minos commissioned his master craftsman, Daedalus, to construct a labyrinth from which the Minotaur could never escape. In order to feed the beast, Minos called in a debt owed to him by King Aegeus of Athens, compelling him to supply a regular tribute of seven Athenian youths and seven virgins, who would be sent into the labyrinth to be devoured by the voracious Minotaur.

When the third sacrificial tribute was due, Aegeus' own son, Theseus, volunteered to take part—and to kill off the Minotaur once and for all. Upon arrival in Crete, he caught the attention of Ariadne, Minos's daughter, who vowed to help him survive his mission. But it was only thanks to the intervention of Daedalus, who gave Theseus directions and a ball of thread with which to mark his route back, that the Minotaur was duly slain.

Theseus departed triumphantly, abandoning Ariadne on his way home to Athens, while Daedalus found himself imprisoned in the labyrinth he himself had designed—and from which his winged escape with his son, Icarus, ended in well-known tragedy.

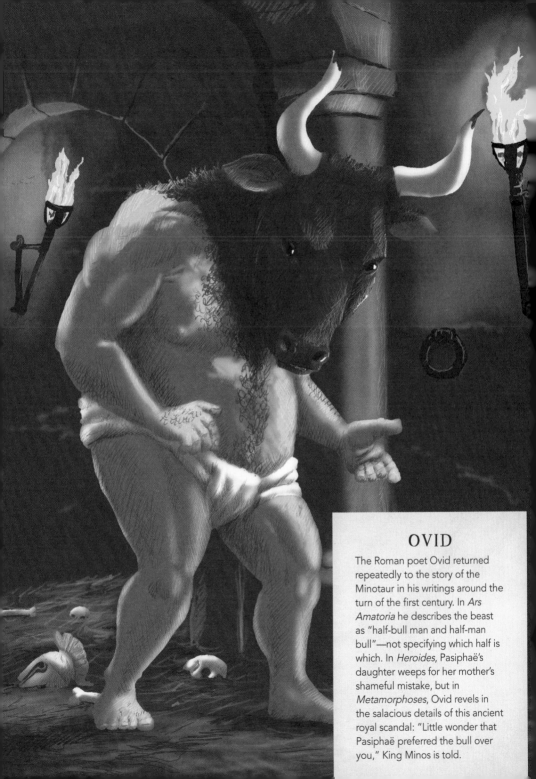

OVID

The Roman poet Ovid returned repeatedly to the story of the Minotaur in his writings around the turn of the first century. In *Ars Amatoria* he describes the beast as "half-bull man and half-man bull"—not specifying which half is which. In *Heroides*, Pasiphaë's daughter weeps for her mother's shameful mistake, but in *Metamorphoses*, Ovid revels in the salacious details of this ancient royal scandal: "Little wonder that Pasiphaë preferred the bull over you," King Minos is told.

LEGENDS OF AWESOMENESS

The wise and ancient qilin made a surprise cameo appearance in *Legends of Awesomeness*, the television spin-off series to DreamWorks' award-winning feature film *Kung Fu Panda*. In an episode entitled "Qilin Time," kung fu student Po hears his father boast of being attacked by a murderous qilin—and goes in search of the creature himself. The fearsome monster is revealed to be nothing but a misunderstood chef, who returns to Po's village to boost sales at his father's noodle shop.

QILIN

The wise and noble qilin is a bringer of good fortune and a herald of great wisdom—for those lucky enough to receive a visit.

Most mythical creatures, though fascinating to behold from afar, would be alarming to encounter face to face. Not so the Chinese qilin (kirin in Japan), which only appears in the presence of a wise or important person. Legend has it that a qilin foretold the future greatness of Confucius by visiting his pregnant mother in the sixth century BCE, although the first recorded sighting was some two thousand years earlier, in the garden of the (subsequently great) Yellow Emperor.

Qilin are peaceful, benevolent, and perfectly balanced creatures; the name is a combination of *qi* ("male") and *lin* ("female"). They are imposing but never hostile: an oft-quoted attribute is their ability to walk on grass without crushing it underfoot. They punish the wicked and bring good luck to those who deserve it.

THE CHINESE UNICORN

Seeing a qilin is an honor beyond compare, but whether one would recognize it is another matter. The qilin is a hybrid creature that is generally described as having the body parts of various other animals: the head of a lion, the body of a deer, the hooves of a horse, the tail of an ox, and the scales of a fish. It is a horned beast, but whether it has a single alicorn (like a unicorn) or a pair of antlers (like a deer) varies from one account to the next. It is also liable to be aglow with golden flames.

The Ming emperor Yongle was presented with what was supposed to be a qilin in 1414. Although he had never seen one in the flesh, even he could tell that the East African giraffe standing before him was nothing of the sort, but this did not prevent the two beasts from becoming connected in the popular imagination. In Japanese, "kirin" can mean either "Chinese unicorn" or "giraffe."

Satyrs

Wild creatures of the forest, satyrs spurn work and warfare in favor of drunken frolics with their female friends.

L ike centaurs, satyrs are part man, part horse; but unlike centaurs they are neither ferocious nor principled.

Satyrs have the body of a strong, virile man with an equine tail and ears. As adherents of Dionysus (Roman Bacchus), the Greek god of wine and fertility, they enjoy nothing more than a wild and drunken party surrounded by beautiful maenads—the god's equally intoxicated female followers. Peaceful and work-shy, satyrs are often pictured carrying a thyrsus, a staff topped with a pinecone, which is used in ritual dances—or carried as a weapon by maenads wanting to repel the advances of lusty satyrs.

Ancient Greek dramatists developed an entire branch of theater around these carefree creatures, with surviving "satyr plays" including Sophocles' *Icheutnae*, Aeschylus' *Net Fishers*, and Euripides' *Cyclops*.

PAN'S PIPES

The Romans conflated the Greek satyr with their own mythical beast-man of the woods, the faun, who has the upper body of a man with the legs and horns of a goat. Fauns are rather more sedate than their Greek counterparts, foregoing wine and seduction in favor of watching over forests and herds in reverence to the woodland deity Faunus.

In the Greek tradition, Faunus's equivalent is the pipe-player Pan. Although he more closely resembles a faun than a satyr, Pan, as god of the wild and a symbol of fertility, is a bridge between the two species. His famous pipes were born of heartbreak: having fallen in love with a beautiful nymph named Syrinx, Pan chased her to the bank of a river, where her sisters transformed her into a reed. Pan was unable to recognize which reed was his true love, but the wind blowing through them made an intoxicating sound. He fashioned his pipes from seven of the reeds and named the instrument a syrinx.

THE LION, THE WITCH AND THE WARDROBE

A friendly faun is the first creature Lucy Pevensie encounters when she accidentally wanders into Narnia in C. S. Lewis's *The Lion, the Witch and the Wardrobe*. Greeting her in a snowy forest, Mr Tumnus takes her back to his woodland home, where he feeds her and plays enchanting, soporific music on his pipe. But instead of trapping her, as the law of Narnia under the White Witch dictates, Tumnus chooses to help the Pevensie children restore Aslan to glory.

THE TEN COMMANDMENTS

Legendary Hollywood filmmaker Cecil B. DeMille broke box-office records with his 1923 silent epic *The Ten Commandments*, the first production to cost more than $1 million to make. Without special effects, he had to build background scenery to scale—including twenty-one plaster sphinx sculptures that were transported to the sand dunes of California. Removing them again was so costly that, like the Great Sphinx of Giza, they were simply left at the mercy of the wind and sand. In 2012, archaeologists used the film to locate the statues, which were finally uncovered in 2014 and removed for display.

Sphinxes

Benign or bloodthirsty, the sphinx has two distinctly different characters depending on whether it is Egyptian or Greek.

With the head of a human and the body of a lion, sphinxes are regal-looking mythical beasts that are most commonly associated with ancient Egypt. There, in statue form, they traditionally guard the tombs of the pharaohs.

What we know about Egyptian sphinxes is almost entirely deduced from the relatively few remaining sphinx statues, among them the Alabaster Sphinx of Memphis—carved in around 1500 BCE—and most famously the Great Sphinx of Giza, dating to around 2500 BCE. That the faces of these sphinx sculptures are thought to be modeled on the pharaoh whose tomb they adorn is indicative of the high veneration in which these beasts were held. One theory for this choice of symbolic creature is that its combination of human and lion suggested a comparison between the deceased pharaoh and the great goddess Sekhmet, who was usually depicted as a lion, or a woman with a lion's head.

The Great Sphinx, measuring approximately 241 feet (73 meters) in length and 66 feet (20 meters) in height, was most likely constructed for the pharaoh Khafra, who was interred in one of the three pyramids nearby. Always at the mercy of windblown sand, by 1400 BCE the Sphinx had become submerged up to its neck. A young prince, Thutmose, came across it while out hunting and stopped for a rest in its shadow; the Sphinx appeared to him in a dream and promised Thutmose that he would become the next pharaoh if he excavated and restored its body. This he did, and duly became Thutmose IV.

THE RIDDLE OF THE SPHINX

The Egyptians did not call these beasts "sphinxes," and what they did call them is unknown. The ancient Greeks, who saw a similarity between the Egyptian human-lion hybrid and their own mythical sphinx, which had the head of a woman and the body of a lion, as well as the wings of an eagle and a serpent for a tail, applied the name sphinx. The word is thought to come from the Greek verb *sphingein*, "to squeeze" or "to strangle," because lionesses strangle their prey to death.

In Greek mythology, the sphinx guarded the gates to the great city of Thebes. She sat high on a rock and posed a riddle to anyone who wanted to pass her; if she did not receive a satisfactory answer she would swoop down to strangle and devour the hapless traveler. This proved a rather one-sided arrangement, because nobody was able to answer the sphinx's most enigmatic riddle: What walks on four legs in the morning, two legs at noon, and three legs in the evening? Oedipus was the first to deduce the answer: Man, who crawls on all fours in childhood, walks upright as an adult, and uses a walking stick in old age. Incandescent with rage that someone had thwarted her, the sphinx threw herself off her rock and was destroyed. The grateful people of Thebes, free at last, made Oedipus their king.

> NOBODY WAS ABLE TO ANSWER THE SPHINX'S MOST ENIGMATIC RIDDLE: WHAT WALKS ON FOUR LEGS IN THE MORNING, TWO LEGS AT NOON, AND THREE LEGS IN THE EVENING?

THE MAN-EATER

At first glance, the manticore of Persian legend appears to bear great similarity to the Egyptian sphinx, having the body of a red lion and a (horned) human head, but there the likeness ends. Unlike the gentle Egyptian sphinx, the manticore ("man-eater") is a terrifying and bloodthirsty monster. It has three rows of sharp teeth and uses a strangely alluring call—a sound somewhere between a trumpet and a flute—to draw its victims near. In his *Natural History* of the first century CE, Roman historian Pliny the Elder lists the manticore among the real-life animals of Ethiopia. "It is blood-colored," he writes, "with a tail ending in a sting, like a scorpion's…and it has a particular appetite for human flesh." The manticore was said to use its scorpion tail to paralyze its victims before swallowing them whole.

UNICORNS

Beautiful and magical but capable of great ferocity, the elusive unicorn has survived a checkered past to become the noblest of mythical beasts.

Ask anyone to draw a unicorn and they will conjure up an image of a gleaming white horse with a lustrous mane and a single spiral horn. Rainbows may feature heavily, for unicorns are known to be the benevolent peace-bringers of the mythical world. But this image is the result of many centuries' evolution: the earliest descriptions of unicorns are surprisingly frightening.

The Roman polymath Pliny the Elder mentions the mythical beast in his ten-volume encyclopedia, *Natural History*, which was published in the first century CE. Describing what he called a "monoceros" ("one horn"), Pliny warns that it is "the most furious beast," with a fearsome deep cry. Horse-like in shape, the monoceros has the head of a stag, the feet of an elephant, the tail of a boar, and an enormous black horn in the middle of its forehead. "This wild beast," he writes, "cannot possibly be caught alive."

MONSTERS AND MAIDENS

Pliny was not the first writer to describe the unicorn—accounts from ancient Egypt refer to a multicolored donkey with a purple head and a horn of red, white, and black—but Pliny brought the elusive beast to a wide audience. As handwritten copies of his influential encyclopedia gradually made their way to other parts of Europe, the myth of the unicorn became established fact. The creatures even crop up a number of times in certain versions of the Bible, although scholars suspect that the Hebrew word *re'em* was mistranslated as "unicorn" when it in fact referred to the aurochs, a non-mythical but long-extinct ancestor of the cow.

By the seventh century, the unicorn had still not lost its terrifying reputation: it had no fear of elephants, according to the religious scholar Isidore of Seville,

UNICORNS IN NARNIA AND HARRY POTTER

Since receiving their much-needed boost in popularity in the early Middle Ages, unicorns have consistently been used in art and literature to symbolize virtue and purity. While C. S. Lewis portrays them as friends and loyal supporters of Aslan in *The Chronicles of Narnia*, J. K. Rowling emphasizes the wickedness of her most evil character through his mistreatment of unicorns. In order to regain his strength and fuel his return to power, Voldemort drinks unicorn blood in the first book of the Harry Potter series—caring little for the curse that will befall him for slaying such a noble beast.

and would quite happily kill one with its horn. Isidore explained that the unicorn was far too strong to be captured by hunters, supporting Pliny's explanation for why almost nobody had ever seen one, but he did offer one clever way of catching a unicorn alive: simply put a virgin girl in its path, breasts bared, and the vicious beast will immediately become calm enough to trap. In some tales of such encounters, the maiden is explicitly used to represent the Virgin Mary and the unicorn the innocence of Christ.

Between them, these myths of a nobler, more peaceful beast inspired many centuries of heraldic symbols and religious artworks, and gradually the unicorn went from monstrous to magnificent.

THE MAGICAL ALICORN

In the Middle Ages, unicorns were so in vogue that vast riches would be exchanged for so-called unicorn horn—or alicorn—which was thought to possess numerous magical properties. Many apothecaries sold what they claimed was ground alicorn powder that could counteract poison, protect against plagues, purify water, whiten teeth, cure most maladies, and act as a powerful aphrodisiac.

Monarchs were particularly keen to get their hands on alicorn, or anything that resembled it. Queen Elizabeth I treasured a horn presented to her in 1577 by the explorer Martin Frobisher, while King Frederick III of Denmark went one step further and had his entire throne fashioned from what looks like alicorn but is in fact narwhal tusk. In Scotland, the unicorn was adopted as a royal emblem as far back as the twelfth century, and today still features alongside the English lion on the United Kingdom's royal coat of arms.

> PLINY'S UNICORN HAD THE HEAD OF A STAG, THE FEET OF AN ELEPHANT, THE TAIL OF A BOAR, AND AN ENORMOUS BLACK HORN.

THE UNICORN OF THE SEA

While skeptics claim that ancient unicorn sightings were in fact rhinoceroses—which may account for the black horn and elephant-killing tendencies—the real-life creature most commonly associated with the unicorn is the narwhal, a bizarre-looking member of the whale family that inhabits Arctic waters. The male's single spiral horn is in fact a long canine tooth. Herman Melville referred to the beast as the "unicorn whale" in *Moby-Dick*, while Jules Verne described "the unicorn of the sea" as having brought great destruction to large whales and ships alike.

CHAPTER 5

HUMANOID CREATURES

Few fantastical beings are more unnerving than those that resemble humans: they look like us, or a version of us, and yet possess grotesque features, brute strength, or potent magical powers. Some of them, like werewolves and witches, use their physical or supernatural advantage for evil. Others, including trolls and cyclopes, are less cunning: they have plenty of brawn but lack the brain to outwit their opponents. The yeti, meanwhile, forever pursued across the Himalayas by generations of trophy-hunting explorers, just wants to be left alone.

Cyclopes

A brutal race of one-eyed giants, Cyclopes are ruthless, savage, and hungry for human flesh.

With a name meaning "round eye," Cyclopes are a tribe of ferocious one-eyed giants who feed on human flesh. The most famous is Polyphemus, the godless Cyclops encountered by Ulysses in Homer's *Odyssey*, but the concept of Cyclopes had existed in a number of earlier Greek legends. The *Theogony* by Hesiod, a poet thought to be a near contemporary of Homer's, credits three Cyclopes brothers with forging the thunderbolts that helped Zeus and the gods of Mount Olympus to overthrow their predecessors, the Titans.

Where the ancient Greeks found inspiration for the Cyclops myth is unknown, but paleontologists have put forward a theory that it could have been the unearthed skulls of a long-extinct species of European elephant, whose nasal cavity was misinterpreted as a single enormous eye socket.

THE X-MEN

Homer's Cyclops may be a man-eating monster, but in 1963 Cyclops were given a welcome PR boost by Marvel Comics, which made Cyclops one of the five founding members of the X-Men, mutants with superhuman skills who fight for justice and peace. Cyclops can neutralize enemies and whole structures using optic blasts from his eye, making him both a useful weapon and incredibly popular with the ladies. By the 1970s, he had become the leader of the team.

ULYSSES AND THE CYCLOPS

On his return to Ithaca from the Trojan War, Ulysses and his men land on the island of the Cyclopes to gather supplies. On finding a cave filled with cheeses and meats, they set up camp and await the return of the cave's inhabitant. When Polyphemus arrives and sees the men, he eats them for breakfast, dashing their brains against the ground and gobbling up "flesh, bones, marrow, and entrails." After plying the giant with wine until he is sick, wily Ulysses blinds his host by driving a burning stake into his eye. He is then able to sneak away, leaving Polyphemus to cry out to his jeering fellow Cyclopes.

GIANTS

Intimidating, strong, loud, and fearsome, giants eat humans by the fistful—but are easily outwitted.

Giants are superhuman—a taller, stronger, hungrier version of mankind—but thanks to a woefully low level of intelligence, their history is a sorry tale of failure after failure. Height and strength aside, giants vary in appearance and status: some, like the Cyclops, are one-eyed; some are simple sons of the Earth while others are the sons of mighty gods. All giants are single-mindedly power-hungry—but without the brains to match their brawn, they all get their comeuppance in the end.

GIANTS VERSUS HEROES

In many mythologies, giants ruled the world before the gods rose to supremacy. In the Old Testament, the Philistine giant Goliath fights with David—ancestor of Jesus Christ and future king of Israel—and is knocked out by a stone before having his head chopped off. In Greek mythology, the Gigantes, sons of Uranus ("Heaven") and Gaia ("Earth"), fought Zeus and the Olympian gods for celestial dominance—and were all slain. In Norse mythology, the primeval giant Ymir likewise preceded the "true" gods, among them Odin and his brothers, who killed Ymir and created the Earth from his flesh and the seas from his blood.

GIANTS ARE SINGLE-MINDEDLY POWER-HUNGRY—BUT WITHOUT THE BRAINS TO MATCH THEIR BRAWN, THEY ALL GET THEIR COMEUPPANCE IN THE END.

In around 1136, an English bishop named Geoffrey of Monmouth published his fantastical *History of the Kings of Britain*, a pseudo-historical chronicle that begins with the triumphant arrival in Britain of the great Trojan warriors Corineus and Brutus and culminates in the exploits of King Arthur and the wizard Merlin. Among the trials supposedly faced by the conquering Trojans was the defeat of Britain's native giants, the most indefatigable of whom was Gogmagog. Finally, Corineus challenged Gogmagog to a fight, during which he found his own superhuman strength, threw the giant over his shoulder and ran to the nearest cliff, from which he flung him into the sea.

In an alternative version of the same legend, Gog and Magog were the last two survivors of a race of British giants. They were taken to London and chained to the gates of a palace that stood on the site of today's Guildhall. Since the fifteenth century, Guildhall has been home to a succession of effigies of these "Guardians of the City of London."

BEANS AND TURNIPS

With their tremendous size and rapacious hunger, and their partiality to senseless rage, giants have played the role of villain in countless tales and legends. The most famous of them, *Jack and the Beanstalk*, began life in 1734 as *The Story of Jack Spriggins and the Enchanted Bean*. In this early version, young Jack plants a magic bean stolen from his grandmother, an enchantress, and it sprouts into a mile-high stalk. At the top of it lives "the giant Gogmagog," who picks his teeth with enormous trees, has "a bowl of punch as big as St Paul's" and a tobacco box "about the size of Westminster Hall." The better-known version of the story sees Jack accept the magic beans in exchange for the family cow, much to his mother's consternation. In a series of visits to the realm at the top of the beanstalk, Jack ensures his own "happily ever after" by stealing a bag of gold coins, a golden-egg-laying goose, and a self-playing harp—and then chops down the beanstalk when the giant comes after him.

The Giant Mountains on the border of Poland and the Czech Republic are so named because they are said to be home to Rübezahl, a fickle giant who can be friendly one moment and murderous the next, and who, like Jack's giant, is easily outwitted. In one story, Rübezahl kidnaps a Polish princess to become his wife, but she is dreadfully homesick. He tries to appease her with turnips, which she has a magic ability to transform into courtiers and friends—until they wither and rot. One day she sends Rübezahl out to count the turnips, and escapes while he struggles with his arithmetic. Rübezahl means "turnip counter."

THE BFG

When orphan Sophie is snatched from her bed by a giant hand in the dead of night, she doesn't realize how lucky she is. Her captor is the BFG—Big Friendly Giant—who in Roald Dahl's novel of the same name is the only kind giant in all of Giant Country. The BFG has the power to create happy dreams—but also terrible nightmares, and he uses one of these to forewarn the Queen of England that the wicked giants, among them the Fleshlumpeater and the Bloodbottler, must be captured and imprisoned.

OGRES

They are descended from gods, or giant kings, or villainous
French aristocrats...so where did it all go wrong?

O gres have long struggled to escape their reputation as the poor
cousins of giants, but with one notable exception (see panel), have
not succeeded. Like giants they are tall, strong, and can crush
most obstacles with their hairy, ugly feet. The trouble is, ogres are
immensely stupid.

This is not to belittle the skill of ogres in pursuing their favorite pastime:
killing and eating humans, with babies being a particular ogre delicacy. But
although there have been controversial scholarly attempts to interpret certain
more enlightened monsters—among them Beauty's Beast—as distant members
of the ogre family, the popular image of ogres as large, lumbering, inarticulate,
club-carrying, semi-clad, swamp-dwelling brutes has not changed for centuries.

ILLUSTRIOUS ANCESTORS
The name "ogre" has only existed since 1697, when French writer Charles
Perrault published *Histoires ou contes du temps passé*, a collection of centuries
old European fairy tales that he had adapted for a modern audience. Among the
stories, three tales feature ogres: "Puss in Boots," "Sleeping Beauty," and
"Hop-o'-My-Thumb" all contain ill-mannered (if mysteriously wealthy) ogres
and their equally boorish womenfolk, ogresses. In a footnote, Perrault defines
them simply as "wild men who eat little children." Exactly where he found
inspiration for the term "ogre" is unknown, although there are two compelling
theories: Og, King of Bashan, described in the Torah and the Bible as the last of
the giants; and Orcus, a giant god of the Underworld in Roman mythology, who
was also the inspiration for J. R. R. Tolkien's Orcs.

SHREK

When William Steig wrote *Shrek!*, a picture book about an ugly green ogre who accidentally becomes a hero, he could little have foreseen its future. But eleven years later, DreamWorks released the Oscar-winning first film in its extraordinarily successful Shrek series. Disturbed from his solitary swamp life by a gaggle of uninvited fairy-tale characters, Shrek—whose name means "Fright" in Yiddish—ends up on a quest to save Princess Fiona, only to discover that she is secretly an ogress.

TROLLS

Ferocious trolls are the Scandinavian equivalent of giants or ogres. They come in many shapes and sizes, but they all have one thing in common—their hideous appearance.

Depending on the particular story, trolls vary greatly in height, from huge mountain-dwelling monsters to human-sized creatures that lurk in caves to dwarf-like beings that hide beneath rocks. Hairy, lumbering, and incredibly hostile, trolls are afflicted with one fatal flaw: they turn to stone when they are exposed to sunlight. For this reason, they only come out to hunt at night, and they need to live in dark places such as caves and forests or under bridges.

Cave trolls in particular are hoarders of treasure, and since no right-thinking human would ever try to steal from a troll, they only have their fellow trolls to fight off. They generally live and travel in family packs and possess the belligerence to match their brute strength. Because they are as dim-witted as they are strong, trolls spend much of their time in a hotheaded rage.

When they do interact with humans, trolls are thought to be thieves—of possessions as well as of small children and unprotected maidens. Trows, their nocturnal cousins on the Shetland and Orkney islands off the north coast of Scotland, take a surprising delight in music and are particularly keen to kidnap musicians. There is little hope of escape once snatched by a troll: they have an unhealthy appetite for human flesh.

> **TROLLS TURN TO STONE WHEN EXPOSED TO SUNLIGHT, SO THEY ONLY COME OUT TO HUNT AT NIGHT AND NEED TO LIVE IN DARK PLACES, SUCH AS CAVES AND FORESTS OR UNDER BRIDGES.**

SCANDINAVIAN ORIGINS

The word "troll" comes from an Old Norse word describing a non-human giant or monster. It also carries with it a supernatural element: in Swedish, *trolla* means "to bewitch," while *trolleri* means "magic." Trolls appear in numerous myths and fairy tales, the most famous of which, *The Three Billy Goats Gruff*, first appeared in an 1845 anthology of traditional Norwegian folk stories collected by Peter Christen Asbjørnsen and Jørgen Moe. As is common in troll tales, it serves to poke fun at the creatures' extreme stupidity.

Three ravenous goats have run out of food on their side of a stream and must cross to the other side, where the grass is quite literally greener. There is a bridge, but beneath it lives a fearsome and hideous troll—and the troll is hungry, too. When he hears the clip-clop of the smallest goat's hooves, he threatens to come up and swallow him whole. The goat protests that he is far too little to make a decent meal, and promises that a much bigger goat will be along shortly. The second goat duly appears, is likewise menaced by the troll, and likewise promises that a much bigger goat is following just behind. When the biggest goat comes clomping over the bridge, the troll is in no mood for further idle threats. He jumps up to claim his bounty, but the goat attacks first, poking out the troll's eyes with his horns and headbutting him into the water. All three goats saunter off for the finest feast of their lives.

PEER GYNT

Also among Asbjørnsen and Moe's collection of Norwegian fairy tales was *Per Gynt*, the story of a feckless youth who runs away to the mountains and there encounters a host of devil-like trolls at the court of the Mountain King. It inspired Henrik Ibsen, Norway's greatest playwright, to compose his 1867 work *Peer Gynt*, which benefited from the subsequent addition of an iconic musical score by Edvard Grieg.

In the best-known piece from the play, "In the Hall of the Mountain King"— an eerie, echoing, ominous evocation of the troll king's lair—the horde of hideous courtiers implore their king to slay Peer, to bite him, and hack off his fingers and pull out his hair before roasting him on a spit. The king has other ideas, however, and fancies Peer as a potential suitor to his daughter. At first intrigued, Peer makes a narrow escape—only to be pursued across the mountains by the troll princess, who informs him that her horribly deformed half-troll child is Peer's offspring, which has been conceived through the power of his lustful mind.

TROLLHUNTER

In André Øvredal's fantasy "mockumentary," *Trollhunter*, from 2010, a group of Norwegian film students head into the mountains on the trail of a suspected poacher. There they make the terrifying discovery that he does not track bears, as previously thought, but rather man-eating trolls. True to the traditions of Scandinavian folklore, these enormous creatures are highly susceptible to light, which turns them to stone and can even cause them to explode. The students join the hunt, and at one point successfully lure a troll by herding three billy goats onto a bridge.

WEREWOLVES

In the dead of night, when the full moon shines brightly, listen for a telltale bloodcurdling howl: a werewolf might be on the loose.

H alf man and half wolf—the name literally means "man-wolf" in Old English—werewolves can look perfectly normal when in their human form. But once a month, beneath a full moon, their skin becomes bristly, their fangs and claws come out, and they stalk the shadows hunting for fresh meat.

Belief in lycanthropy—the ability to transform into a wolf—may have stemmed from ancient European warriors donning wolf skins as part of a hunting ritual. Certainly by the time of the ancient Greek civilization, the idea of temporary transformation existed. Writing in the fifth century BCE, the historian Herodotus describes a faraway tribe whose members "turn into a wolf for a few days once a year, and then go back to their original form."

Although some werewolves are able to transform at will, most are at the mercy of the moon; and while lycanthropy is a hereditary condition, it can also be passed on by a werewolf's bite. However and whenever the transformation occurs, it wears off completely as soon as the sun comes up.

A GREEDY, DEVOURING WOLF

During the mass hysteria about witches in Medieval Europe, which saw tens of thousands of women tried and executed for sorcery, accusations of lycanthropy were also widespread. Werewolf trials began in what is now Switzerland in the 1420s but quickly radiated across Central Europe;

TEEN WOLF

A high school student who longs to stand out from the crowd gets more than he bargained for in the 1985 film *Teen Wolf*. Scott Howard, played by Michael J. Fox, is initially alarmed when he transforms into a werewolf one night—only to discover that his father is also touched by this family curse. Scott uses his alter ego to become the most popular boy in school, but a moment of brute violence turns him from hero to freak. Ultimately he must learn how to rely on his own merit, rather than the werewolf's strength, in order to stand out.

the last recorded trial and execution was in Austria in 1725. In some cases it took little more than a missing child for the authorities to incite a werewolf hunt. Like suspected witches, suspected werewolves were often tortured to extract a confession, and once convicted they were burned at the stake.

In 1573 the so-called "Werewolf of Dôle," Gilles Garnier, explained at trial that a strange ointment that turned him into a wolf had caused his cannibalistic rampage. In Maastricht in 1605, three men confessed to having killed and eaten a child while under the influence of their lupine alter egos. Later that century in Estonia, "Hans the Werewolf" told prosecutors that a mysterious man in black had given him the ability to turn into a wolf, and that he was incapable of rational thought while transformed. One of the most notorious trials was that of Peter Stumpf, the "Werewolf of Bedburg" in Germany, in 1589. Stumpf was the perpetrator of a series of horrific cannibalizations, targeting women, children, and cattle, which at his trial he attributed to the effects of a wolf skin belt given to him by the devil himself. Wearing the belt turned him into "a greedy, devouring wolf." His torture and execution were almost as grizzly as his own crimes: he was torn limb from limb before being beheaded and burned.

ONCE A MONTH, BENEATH A FULL MOON, THEIR SKIN BECOMES BRISTLY, THEIR FANGS AND CLAWS COME OUT, AND THEY STALK THE SHADOWS HUNTING FOR FRESH MEAT.

SILVER BULLETS

With their ferocious strength and superhuman speed, werewolves are fairly impervious to injury. In some legends they are repelled by wolfsbane; in others this flowering plant even has the potency to bring them permanently back to their human form. Exorcism can likewise neutralize a werewolf's lupine tendencies. But if attacked while not in the presence of a priest, there is only one way to kill the creature: silver. Silver bullets are said to be particularly effective, but silver canes, blades, and arrows work, too. This belief was inspired by the fate of the so-called "Beast of Gévaudan," an enormous wolf or werewolf held responsible for at least 100 gruesome massacres in France in the 1760s. Terror of the beast was so widespread that King Louis XV stepped in and dispatched his finest sharpshooters to hunt it down and slay it. After many months and more brutal deaths, it was a silver bullet fired by a peasant named Jean Chastel that ended the Beast of Gévaudan's murderous spree.

Witches

"Double, double toil and trouble; fire burn, and cauldron bubble..." Witches' wicked spells bring grotesque transformations and even death to their enemies.

Witches are enchanted old crones who use their sorcery for evil. With their pointy hats, black cats, bubbling cauldrons, and flying broomsticks—not to mention their shrieking cackles and hideous warty noses—witches have a hard time staying incognito. It is not impossible, however; in Roald Dahl's *The Witches* (1983), a cunning disguise involving wigs, gloves, and shoes hides the fact that these witches are hairless and toeless with ugly clawed hands.

Ugliness is almost universal among witches. In L. Frank Baum's *Wonderful Wizard of Oz* (1900), the Wicked Witch of the West is described as a one-eyed hag with hordes of evil winged creatures at her disposal. For the 1939 film she developed green skin, a feature that has since become common in depictions of witches. In *Hansel and Gretel*, published in 1812 by the Brothers Grimm, the witch is a cruel, withered, red-eyed old woman who lures children to her house made of gingerbread and sugar. In Shakespeare's *Macbeth*, written in around 1600, the three witches who plot Macbeth's murderous ascension to the throne are "so wither'd and so wild in their attire," with "skinny lips" and beards, that they "look not like the inhabitants o' the earth."

WITCH-FINDERS

Witchcraft has been feared since at least the early Middle Ages. Alfred the Great, King of Wessex in the ninth century, specifically outlawed witchcraft, which was by then already associated only with women despite the word's origins in the Old English "wicca": "(male) sorcerer." It is not clear when or why witches adopted their cats, hats, and broomsticks; possibly these were simply accessories common to the sort of lonely old woman who was eyed with suspicion by her neighbors.

THE WORST WITCH

Mildred Hubble is a witch who is not cut out for the job. As a pupil of Miss Cackle's Academy for Witches, the antihero of Jill Murphy's *Worst Witch* books proves a catastrophically inept sorceress. Her spells go wrong, her broomstick malfunctions, and instead of a majestic black cat she has a nervous little tabby. But Mildred always manages to save the day, and in her first term foils a plot hatched by a group of wicked witches, by transforming them into snails and taking them to Miss Cackle for punishment.

By the later Middle Ages, witches were so feared that they were relentlessly sought out and often burned at the stake as heretics. One of the earliest recorded cases was Alice Kyteler of County Kilkenny in Ireland, who in 1324 was accused of murder, ritualistic animal sacrifice, and sorcery. Although she managed to flee to England, her maidservant was burned at the stake in her place.

From the fourteenth to the eighteenth century, Europe was gripped by hysteria concerning the spread of witchcraft, and high-profile trials took place in Britain, Germany, and Spain. In 1644, Matthew Hopkins declared himself "Witch Finder General" of England, and over the next few years traveled from village to village carrying out hundreds of trials and executions. The accused women were tortured in order to extract "confessions." "Ducking" was thought to be a particularly effective test for witchcraft: in the belief that witches and water did not mix— witches having renounced the sanctity of their baptism—the accused woman would be thrown into a pond. If she floated, she was a witch and must be executed; if she sank she was innocent, albeit drowned.

> MACBETH'S WITCHES ARE "SO WITHER'D AND SO WILD IN THEIR ATTIRE," WITH "SKINNY LIPS" AND BEARDS, THAT THEY "LOOK NOT LIKE THE INHABITANTS O' THE EARTH."

THE SALEM WITCH TRIALS

Witch panic may have started in Europe, but the most notorious witch trials occurred in the US. In 1692, there were reports of strange goings-on at the home of Samuel Parris, the pastor of Salem Village (now Danvers) in Massachusetts. His daughter and niece had begun suffering fits, screaming and contorting, and being menaced by invisible forces, and it was clear to the townsfolk that witchcraft was to blame. Scientists now believe that they experienced hallucinations brought on by bread infected with the fungus ergot. When asked who had bewitched them, the girls accused the family servant and two local outcasts, who were put on trial and pressured into incriminating themselves and each other. This only served to convince the people of Salem that the town was under sustained attack, and dozens more women suffered fits or were accused of witchcraft. The governor of Massachusetts stepped in and established a court to try Salem's witches, and over the course of a year, nineteen people were found guilty and hanged. It was only when the governor's wife found herself in the spotlight that the trials were brought to a close.

Wizards

Wise wizards have the power to conjure spells and see into the future, and are almost always ancient old men— with one very famous exception.

W izards are known by a variety of names—mages, sorcerers, enchanters, and conjurers—all of which refer to the power for which they are best known: they perform spells that are akin to magic. In popular imagination, wizards are often paired with witches, although the two species have very different functions. While most witches use their magical powers for evil, wizards are better known for performing spells that bring good fortune or save lives. The word "wizard," after all, comes from "wise." It is perhaps as a result of this etymology that wizards are usually pictured as philosophical old men, with long flowing beards and a library of dusty old books. They may have an equally wise owl as a companion. Wizards generally wear long academic gowns, with a pointed hat in which they can conjure up spells, and many of them rely on a magic wand or staff.

Druids may have been the earliest wizards. Until the Romans swept through Europe in the first century BCE, these wise old men were revered members of ancient Celtic communities. They were learned in astronomy, philosophy, and medicine, and their word was law. Often they performed ritualistic sacrifices in wooded glades, sometimes even making live human sacrifices for the greater good, such as to ensure victory in battle.

THE PHILOSOPHER'S STONE

By the late Middle Ages, wise old philosophers were more likely to have turned their attention to the study of alchemy. The practitioners of this pseudoscience were convinced of the existence of a "philosopher's stone," a magical substance that could cure all diseases, guarantee immortality, and turn worthless metals into gold. At a time when magic and science were barely distinguishable, alchemists were highly revered. In 1558, Queen Elizabeth I employed alchemist

HARRY POTTER AND THE PHILOSOPHER'S STONE

In 1997 a novel was published that would change the face of wizarding forever: *Harry Potter and the Philosopher's Stone*, the first in a seven-part series by J. K. Rowling. Young Harry is told that he is a wizard and packed off to Hogwarts School of Witchcraft and Wizardry, which he soon learns is home to the one and only philosopher's stone: the prized possession of a certain Nicolas Flamel, an immortal, centuries-old alchemist. Evil Lord Voldemort is determined to get his hands on it and ensure his own immortality, and only Harry stands in his way.

John Dee as her astrological adviser, even trusting him to decide on the most auspicious date for her coronation.

In 1612, a mysterious book was published in Paris that was supposedly written by the fourteenth-century French alchemist Nicolas Flamel. In *Exposition of the Hieroglyphical Figures*, Flamel claims to have discovered a strange manuscript that a wandering sage identified as a book of Egyptian alchemical spells. He explains how he used the book's secret incantations to produce the philosopher's stone, with which he was able to create silver and then gold out of ordinary metals, as well as achieve immortality. Flamel supposedly died in 1418, but the story goes that grave robbers later opened his coffin only to find it empty—Flamel having faked his own death so that he could live forever in peace.

> WIZARDS ARE USUALLY PICTURED AS PHILOSOPHICAL OLD MEN, WITH LONG FLOWING BEARDS AND A LIBRARY OF DUSTY OLD BOOKS. THEY MAY HAVE AN EQUALLY WISE OWL AS A COMPANION.

THE SWORD IN THE STONE

Until 1997 (see panel), the most famous wizard in the world had for many centuries been Merlin, adviser to the legendary King Arthur. Based loosely on a visionary wise man named Myrddin—who in Welsh folklore lived among animals in a forest and was able to see into the future—Merlin the wizard first appeared in Geoffrey of Monmouth's inventive *History of the Kings of Britain*, composed in around 1135. He proved so popular a character that many other writers borrowed him for their own Arthurian legends in the twelfth and thirteenth centuries. In some of these, Merlin is said to be the offspring of a demon and a nun, whose baptism at birth eradicated any sinister characteristics he might have inherited from his father.

One famous story recounts Merlin's dedication to the young Arthur, whom he educates and safeguards until the time is right for him to become king. It is only when Arthur frees Excalibur, a sword embedded in stone, which belonged to his late father, that he realizes it is his destiny to become king and unite his country. Merlin gives him a great table and instructs him to assemble a council of the bravest and best warriors in the kingdom, later immortalized as the Knights of the Round Table.

The Yeti

Remote mountain ranges provide the perfect refuge for all sorts of wildlife. But might they harbor something else—something more human than animal?

To the Sherpas of eastern Nepal, the yeti is a long-established facet of Himalayan folklore. In 1991, Nepalese writer and explorer Shiva Dhakal published a collection of oral stories he had collated while traveling through remote Sherpa communities, which revealed for the first time in print the extent to which the legendary yeti is entrenched in Himalayan mythology. The beast was renowned as a vicious flesh-eating monster, an ape-man who could not be outwitted and whom it was terribly bad luck just to see.

To Western explorers, the yeti is still a relatively new discovery, and one that was only made possible by improvements in transport and extreme-terrain hiking equipment in the nineteenth century.

THE ICEMAN COMETH

In 1832, British explorer B. H. Hodgson was trekking through the Himalayas when his local guides suddenly stopped in terror. They had, they claimed, seen an enormous "wild man" dead ahead. (The Tibetan *yeh-teh* is akin to "animal man.") With remarkable stoicism, Hodgson dismissed the sighting as some sort of monkey and in a footnote to his subsequent report on Nepalese wildlife, published in the *Journal of the Asiatic Society of Bengal*, rebuked his men for fleeing instead of shooting. "It moved, they said, erectly," he casually reported, "was covered with long dark hair, and had no tail."

In 1921, Charles Howard-Bury led a British reconnaissance expedition to Mount Everest. In his account of the mission, *Mount Everest: The Reconnaissance, 1921*, he too dismissed the locals' terror of a "bogey man" who left enormous footprints in the snow. He recorded that the local name for this

"wild man of the snow" was Metohkangmi, or the Abominable Snowman. His guides, like Hodgson's almost a century earlier, described a large, bare-footed man covered in long hair.

It was not until 1951 that visual evidence emerged in the form of a photograph apparently showing yeti footprints, taken by mountaineer Eric Shipton. The photographs sparked such a frenzy of interest back in Britain that the *Daily Mail* newspaper mounted its own "Snowman Expedition" in 1954. Its team of explorers found more footprints but more intriguingly they came across a hairy human-like scalp that was kept in a monastery high up in the Himalayas. Tests on the long, reddish-brown hair were inconclusive, but have long been taken by believers to belong to the elusive Abominable Snowman.

> **THE YETI IS RENOWNED AS A VICIOUS FLESH-EATING MONSTER, AN APE-MAN WHO CANNOT BE OUTWITTED AND WHOM IT IS TERRIBLY BAD LUCK JUST TO SEE.**

BIGFOOT

If the yeti is the "wild man of the snow," then Bigfoot, said to roam the remote valleys and forests of the northwestern United States and western Canada, is the "wild man of the woods." And in the near-extinct Salish language historically spoken by local Native Americans, the creature's name, "Sasquatch," means just that. In almost all other respects, the descriptions of the two creatures are remarkably similar.

Bigfoot has been described as an enormously tall ape-man who stands on two feet, and who emits an appalling stench. He has long arms and thick, dark hair all over his body. The first person to record coming across footprints supposedly belonging to Bigfoot, British explorer David Thompson, reported in 1811 that they were 14 inches (35 centimeters) in length and 8 inches (20 centimeters) in breadth. But just like his Himalayan counterparts, Thompson did not believe a word of what his local guides told him. "The Indians would have it to be a young mammoth," he wrote in his journal. He himself felt it could only be "a very large old bear, his claws worn away," but "this the Indians would not allow." Nevertheless, all wisely concurred: "We were in no humor to follow him."

Amateur filmmakers Roger Patterson and Bob Gimlin did choose to follow in 1967, and they shot grainy color footage of a seven-foot creature that seems to tally with the popular description of Bigfoot.

THE ABOMINABLE SNOWMAN

In 1957, at the height of the yeti mania sparked by the *Daily Mail* expedition, Hammer Film Productions brought out a timely film entitled *The Abominable Snowman*. Peter Cushing stars as a botanist drawn, against his better judgment, into a yeti-hunting expedition, during which the photographer, the trapper, and even the Sherpa are picked off by accidents, avalanches, or mortal terror. Cushing is left to face a pack of yeti alone, and comes to see that they are highly intelligent—and have designs to take over the world.

Chapter 6

The Sacred & The Divine

At the pinnacle of the fantastical hierarchy are the deities and sacred beings in this chapter. The mighty Rainbow Serpent created the Earth from deep within the soil of the Australian Outback, and the revered Green Man protects forests and everything in them. Heaven-sent angels and jinn have divine powers that they sometimes misuse, while man-made golems do not know their own strength. The Phoenix is immortal, but for those of us who are not, the Furies and Valkyries are on hand to guide us—the former toward destruction, the latter to eternal glory.

Angels

Wise, loyal, and kind, angels are sent by a greater power
to watch over us, and guide us in all we do.

Angels exist in many of the major world religions, and are usually
depicted as divine messengers. Their name comes from the ancient
Greek *angelos* ("messenger"). More often than not they are humanoid
but winged, an acknowledgment of their function as go-betweens
from heaven to Earth. Traditionally, angels are charged with transporting the
souls of the earthly dead to the relevant celestial resting place; in popular belief,
however, angels are often thought of as actually *being* the souls of the earthly
dead. Both beliefs help explain why angels are described as translucent or
ghostly—they belong to a plane of existence that is literally above and beyond
our mortal world.

The major Abrahamic religions—Judaism, Christianity, and Islam—share
certain beliefs about angels, and a number of named angels appear in all three. The
Mishneh Torah, a book of Jewish religious law compiled in the twelfth century by scholar
and rabbi Moshe Ben Maimon, categorizes the angels into ten ranks. Among them are the
seraphim and cherubim, who in Christianity serve in the first sphere of God's angels. Islam
does not have a hierarchy of angels, but among its few named angels are Jibrail and
Mikhail, who correspond to the Judeo-Christian archangels Gabriel and Michael.

The angel Gabriel is believed by Christians and Muslims to have played a crucial role in
the establishment of both religions. In the Bible he visits the Virgin Mary to tell her that

IT'S A WONDERFUL LIFE

The 1946 film *It's a Wonderful Life*, now a
staple feel-good Christmas classic, begins
most unfestively, with depressed family
man George Bailey (James Stewart)
preparing to commit suicide. Before he
can do so, however, his guardian angel
appears in the form of a wise old man
named Clarence. When George confesses
that he wishes he had never been born,
Clarence shows him an alternate reality in
which that is the case: his town is morally
bankrupt, his business shut down, his wife
a spinster...thanks to Clarence, George
realizes that it's a good life after all.

she will conceive a great son through God and must name him Jesus; the Quran, meanwhile, is said to be the word of Allah transmitted to Mohammed via Gabriel.

GUARDIAN ANGELS

The notion that each person is assigned a guardian angel at birth has existed since at least ancient Greek times. In the fourth century BCE the Greek dramatist Menander wrote: "By every man, as he is born, there stands a spirit good, a holy guide of life."

ANGELS ARE USUALLY DESCRIBED AS TRANSLUCENT OR GHOSTLY; THEY BELONG TO A PLANE OF EXISTENCE THAT IS LITERALLY ABOVE AND BEYOND OUR MORTAL WORLD.

Although people of all faiths and none have historically thanked their guardian angel for helping them in a time of trouble or protecting them from a specific disaster, these angels were popularized by the Abrahamic religions. The Bible is especially rife with references to God sending angels to watch over the faithful; in Psalms, for instance: "There shall no evil befall thee, neither shall any plague come nigh thy dwelling. For he shall give his angels charge over thee, to keep thee in all thy ways." In the Quran, the *al-mu'aqqibat* ("those who follow") are angels commanded by Allah to guard the faithful, one walking in front of a person and the other behind.

VISION QUESTS

Just as guardian angels are believed to watch over and protect a specific person, many Native American tribes have a traditional belief in guardian spirits, which tend to appear in animal form. Although less common now, ritualistic vision quests were once routinely undertaken by adolescents as they moved from childhood to adulthood. These entailed a solitary journey to an isolated location to fast and pray, and ultimately discover and commune with one's spirit animal.

A similar belief associated with Native American tribes—although it exists in a number of ancient cultures across the world—is totemism, the idea that individuals, families, or communities have a sacred spirit animal particular to them. The word "totem" comes from a word used by the North American Ojibwa tribe to indicate "sibling kin." While totems are not usually regarded as deities, they tend to be ascribed supernatural or celestial powers. In tribes from Australia, India, and North America it is highly taboo for members of the same totem family to marry one another, and hunting, harming, or eating one's totem is considered to be akin to hunting, harming, or eating a member of one's family.

The Furies

Hideous, relentless, and hell-bent on serving their skewed form of justice, the Furies are the worst enemy you could ever fear to make.

The genesis of the Furies is as violent as their reputation. According to the *Theogony*, a genealogy of the gods written by the Greek poet Hesiod, the Furies were created when the Titan Cronus castrated his father, Uranus, in an act of revenge. The blood that fell upon the Earth rose up once more in the form of these awe-inspiring goddesses of vengeance.

The Furies—or Erinyes, to give them their Greek name—work as a group, but sources disagree on how big that group is. Traditionally—and largely thanks to Virgil, who specified the number in his *Aeneid*—the dreaded Furies come as a trio: Tisiphone ("Avenger"), Allecto ("Unrelenting"), and Megaera ("Jealous"). These clawed, winged, longhaired sisters are hideous in appearance, and they pursue their victims without mercy. When they emerge from the Underworld, they bring famine and plague upon the Earth.

THE KINDLY ONES

The Furies are so unspeakably terrifying that the ancient Greeks deemed it prudent not even to utter their name, for fear of invoking the goddesses' wrath. Instead they were addressed using euphemisms that meant quite the opposite of Erinyes: usually either the Eumenides ("Kindly Ones") or the Semnai ("Venerable Ones"). The Greek playwrights, Euripides and Aeschylus, near contemporaries in the mid-first millennium BCE, popularized these fawning nicknames. In *Orestes*, Euripides equated the Erinyes with the Eumenides, who had traditionally been known as goddesses of fertility rather than of destruction, while Aeschylus gave his play *The Eumenides* an unlikely happy ending in which the Furies and the Olympian gods make peace with one another.

THE VISIT

In *Orestes* and *The Eumenides*, the Furies torment matricidal Orestes until he is wracked with guilt. The story has inspired countless others, and nowhere to eerier effect than in *The Visit* (1956) by Swiss playwright Friedrich Dürrenmatt. Returning to the village in which she was wronged and rejected, a wealthy old woman promises to bring prosperity to the bankrupt inhabitants—so long as they murder the wrongdoer. When they refuse, she vows that she will wait, and wait, and wait…

GOLEMS

These mindless creatures made from clay will do anything asked of them—but have been known to run riot when left unsupervised.

Its name means "shapeless mass" in Hebrew, and originally a golem was anything incomplete or in an embryonic form. It occurs once in the Bible, in reference to the crude, uncultivated substance fashioned by God into mankind. Adam, the first man, is a golem in that he was created from dust, an inanimate material.

In the Middle Ages, an idea emerged that powerful rabbis might be able to bring inorganic matter magically to life—that they could turn a piece of wood or more often a lump of clay into a humanoid automaton. These soulless, brainless creatures were given the name golem because they were living yet lifeless. Golems are said to be fiercely loyal to the rabbi who created them, carrying out any task without question. The eleventh-century Jewish philosopher Solomon ibn Gabirol, who lived and worked in what is now southern Spain, is credited with having created a female golem to work as his maidservant. When confronted about this sorcery by the Andalusian authorities, he supposedly proved that the woman was simply a creation of his by deconstructing her into her constituent inanimate parts.

TRUTH AND DEATH

The association of golems with rabbis comes from the method of their animation. According to Jewish folklore, a rabbi must write a *shem*—one of the names of God—onto a piece of paper and insert it into the golem's mouth, or write the *shem* across the golem's forehead. The creature can be deactivated either by removing the paper from its mouth, or by rearranging the letters of the *shem* into a word that no longer indicates God. A common legend has golems being brought to life using the Hebrew word *emet* (truth); by removing the first letter, the word becomes *met* (death), and the golem is returned to its inanimate form.

Elijah Ba'al Shem, a sixteenth-century rabbi of Chełm in Poland, is said to have created a golem using the word *emet*. The creature grew to human size and kept on growing, leading the rabbi to fear that it would become big enough to destroy the whole world. In desperation he turned *emet* into *met* in order to deactivate it, but the golem injured him in the process; in some versions of the story, the golem fell on the rabbi and crushed him as it disintegrated into dust.

The most recent report of a golem was in Drohiczyn, Russia, in 1805, where Rabbi David Yaffe created a golem to carry out household chores for him on the Sabbath. The golem would receive his Sabbath instructions a day in advance and then follow them absolutely to the letter. Legend has it that a mistake made by the rabbi when commanding the golem to light a fire instead compelled the creature to burn the whole town to the ground.

> GOLEMS ARE FIERCELY LOYAL TO THE RABBI WHO CREATED THEM. CARRYING OUT ANY TASK WITHOUT QUESTION.

THE GOLEM OF PRAGUE

Judah Löw ben Bezulel, rabbi of Prague in the late sixteenth century, is said to have created the most famous golem in Jewish folklore. The Golem of Prague, also known as Yossele, was fashioned from the clay that lined the banks of the River Vltava, and animated in order to protect the city's Jews from Christian-sponsored persecution. The golem was able to make itself invisible and pass unnoticed, and was given the task of guarding the Jewish ghetto.

The Sabbath was a day of rest for Yossele, and the rabbi would make sure to remove the *shem* from its mouth every Friday evening. But one week he forgot to deactivate the golem and it was left to wander the streets on the Sabbath. In some stories, it went on a violent rampage. Eventually the rabbi caught up with it outside the Old New Synagogue and quickly pulled the *shem* from its mouth, causing the creature to break into pieces. Fearing that it might become a powerful weapon in the wrong hands, the rabbi gathered up the pieces of the golem and locked them away in the attic of the synagogue—where they supposedly remain to this day.

GOLLUM

J. R. R. Tolkien's Gollum, a former hobbit corrupted by greed into a malevolent goblin-like villain, is not strictly a golem—but his name is apt. Gollum lives only for his single-minded pursuit of the One Ring, the sinister "precious" whose dangerous power transformed him into its minion and then kept him in thrall for hundreds of years. The ring is his creator and his controller, and through its sinister lure he reverts to a primitive version of himself: uncultivated, brutish, and solitary. Gollum blindly follows the ring to its—and his own—destruction.

The Green Man

Vast and unexplored, the forest is a place of darkness,
myth, and mystery, home to woodland beings with the
power to control nature.

T he Green Man lives in the forest, but at the same time he *is* the forest: a
woodland spirit present in all vegetation, a symbol of nature and life and
the never-ending cycle of both. Made up entirely of leaves and infused
with ancient wisdom, the Green Man is most commonly depicted as an
ornamental carved "foliate head" on Medieval buildings across Europe, notably
churches. Occasionally, he is festooned with berries or twigs, and sometimes
vegetation is shown flowing from his mouth.

Churches are an unusual place for the Green Man to
appear so prominently, since he is traditionally associated
with pagan beliefs and rituals. As a symbol of man's union
with nature—fertility, birth, life, and death—he serves as
a reminder that mankind relies on nature, is part of
nature, and is ultimately more transient than nature. If
the Green Man "dies," he will return again in the spring.

> THE GREEN
> MAN SERVES AS
> A REMINDER
> THAT MANKIND
> RELIES ON
> NATURE, IS
> PART OF
> NATURE, AND IS
> ULTIMATELY
> MORE
> TRANSIENT
> THAN NATURE.

GODS OF BIRTH AND REBIRTH

The term "Green Man" was coined as recently as 1939,
in an article on English church architecture by Julia
Hamilton, Lady Raglan. But although surviving foliate
heads can be dated back to at least the twelfth century, if
not as far back as the second or third, deities of nature were present in many
ancient mythologies.

Osiris, the Egyptian god of death, the afterlife, and resurrection, was usually
depicted as green-skinned; he was believed to preside over the fertility and
regeneration of nature, as well as the life-giving Nile. The Mesopotamian god
Tammuz oversaw the growth of vegetation and food. In the Babylonian calendar,

the month of Tammuz in midsummer marked the start of a period of mourning for the waning and dying of the year. In the Aztec religion, the god Tlaloc had mastery over water and fertility, life, and food; the volcano Tlalocatepetl was his holiest shrine, and the site of ceremonies that implored—and thanked—him for the rain.

WILD MEN OF THE WOODS

Green men of the forest are popular in folklore. An ancient belief that the passing of the seasons is a battle for supremacy between the Holly King and the Oak King has continued into modern-day paganism. At the summer solstice, the Holly King defeats the Oak King and reigns over the darkening days until the winter solstice, when the Oak King prevails and oversees the return of the sun and new growth.

The spring festival May Day was historically a focus for Green Man customs. In England, a "Jack in the Green," "Green Jack," or "Leaf King" often took part in celebrations between the sixteenth and nineteenth centuries, and in some villages still does. A person covered in leaves and flowers so as to look like a living, walking tree would do a jolly dance through the streets, and even perform practical jokes. In parts of Wales, *Calan Mai* (May 1) was traditionally the day on which the forces of Winter and Summer, festooned with willow and blackthorn respectively, fought a mock battle in which Summer always won.

ROBIN HOOD

In Tudor England, green-clad folk hero Robin Hood became conflated with the Green Man-inspired fertility festivities of spring, starring in many local and even royal celebrations as "King of the May." Although supposedly a real historical figure rather than a woodland deity, Robin Hood has, since his first appearance in ballads in around the fourteenth century, been the predominant folklore guardian of the forests. Living in the trees all year round, Robin Hood is an enemy of selfish man-made laws and hierarchies, living to serve his brand of forest justice to those who set themselves up as superior to it.

John Barleycorn was a symbol of the harvest festival in England in the eighteenth century, although the most popular use of harvested barley—to produce alcoholic drinks—made him a figure of fun rather than reverence. A ballad of 1725 recounts that he "was for the good of mankind born, and therefore…the Commonwealth should drink his blood to nourish health." The Bokwus, a variation on the Green Man who stalks the larch and spruce forests of Canada, is a far less benevolent creature. The silent guardian of every woodland, the Bokwus is only ever glimpsed, briefly, through dense foliage—except by those he chooses to waylay: legend has it that the Bokwus lures unwitting travelers to their watery deaths in tree-lined streams, so that he can take their souls back to his forest home.

JINN

Jinn are magical beings, immensely powerful but inclined to treachery. So be careful what you wish for.

Jinn (or genies) are nowadays probably best known for emerging from magic lamps and granting wishes, but in pre-Islamic Arabia they were known as powerful deities who needed to be appeased in order to bestow good fortune. The Quran explains that they are creations of Allah—formed by him from smokeless fire—and that they live in everything: above and below ground, in flames and air and trees. Jinn eat, marry, and die just like humans but they live much longer. They have free will and can make themselves invisible or take the form of any creature they choose, but they are no less answerable to Allah than all mankind is; on Judgment Day they will be held accountable for their deeds. The Quran says that the great prophet King Solomon was given power over all the jinn on Earth, and used them as slaves in the construction of monuments and places of worship.

> JINN WERE FORMED BY ALLAH FROM SMOKELESS FIRE AND THEY LIVE IN EVERYTHING: ABOVE AND BELOW GROUND, IN FLAMES AND AIR AND TREES.

There are at least three classifications of jinn in Arabic folklore, notably the shape-shifting *ghūl* (ghoul), the witch-like *silā*, and the rebellious *ifrīt*. The Islamic devil, *Iblīs* or *Shaitan*, is a jinni condemned by Allah for refusing to show reverence to Adam.

THE JINNI OF THE LAMP

Scheherazade, the inexhaustible narrator of *The Thousand and One Nights*, which is thought to date back as far as the ninth century, tells a number of stories about jinn. The most famous of them concerns Aladdin, an idle fellow who lives with his poor, widowed mother. One day he is beguiled by a man who claims to be his wealthy uncle—in reality an evil sorcerer—and agrees to help him retrieve a valuable oil lamp from a magical cave. The sorcerer gives him a

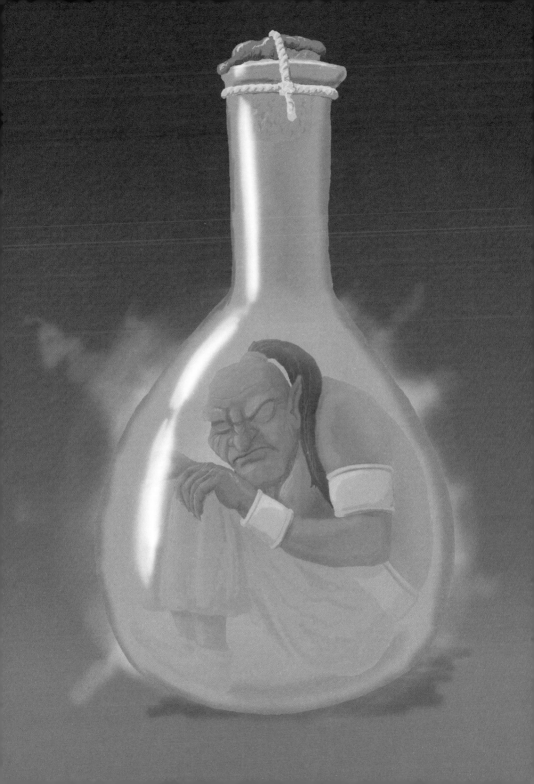

ring that will protect him from harm, but Aladdin becomes suspicious of his supposed uncle, and in a rage the sorcerer traps him in the cave.

Crying and wringing his hands, Aladdin accidentally rubs the ring, and a jinni appears before him. It offers Aladdin a wish, and he asks to be freed from the cave. Before he knows it he is back at his mother's house, holding both the ring and the unremarkable-looking lamp. Planning to sell the latter for food he polishes it, only to have an even mightier jinni appear. It too is able to grant wishes, and Aladdin uses them to become a wealthy suitor to the sultan's daughter. They marry and live in a magnificent palace conjured up by the jinni.

The sorcerer tricks the princess into giving up the lamp so that he can use the jinni for evil, but Aladdin uses the jinni of the ring to wreak his revenge, rescuing the jinni of the lamp and slaying the sorcerer before living happily ever after.

THE FISHERMAN AND THE JINNI

Another tale from Scheherazade is about an old fisherman who has cast his net many times but caught nothing more edible than a dead donkey. He tries one last time and pulls out a strange brass vessel. When he removes the stopper, a huge plume of smoke comes rushing out and forms itself into a very big, very angry jinni. The jinni explains that it had originally vowed to grant its liberator great wealth, but when a century passed without liberation, it downgraded the vow to three wishes; by the time another century had passed, the jinni was absolutely furious. It vowed to kill the man who freed it, but to let him choose the manner of his death.

The fisherman is terrified but devises a plan. Playing to the jinni's vanity, he starts to express doubts that such a great and powerful being could possibly have squeezed into such a small vessel. In a flash of arrogance, the jinni disperses into smoke and shoots back into the bottle—and the fisherman quickly replaces the stopper, trapping the jinni inside.

ALADDIN

Disney's 1992 all-singing, Oscar-winning animation *Aladdin* largely follows the *Thousand and One Nights* original, but features just one larger-than-life genie, voiced by Robin Williams. Offering to grant Aladdin three wishes, the genie lays out some ground rules: he cannot kill anyone, force anyone to fall in love, bring anyone back from the dead, or grant a wish for more wishes. The genie, meanwhile, has his own wish: he wants to be freed from the lamp. But his only hope is for Aladdin to wish him free— and Aladdin has more selfish plans.

The Phoenix

Famous for dying in flames before being reborn, the phoenix is the most dramatic of mythical birds.

The enigmatic phoenix is a bird with a spectacular gift for self-sufficiency and regeneration. Feeding only on droplets of dew, it lives in solitude for many hundreds of years before building a nest of sweet-smelling twigs, setting light to them, and going up in flames on the pyre. But then, from the smoldering ashes, it rises once again, reborn into yet another new life as the world's only phoenix.

HISTORICAL HAGGLING

Classical historians were fascinated by accounts of the phoenix, which they believed originated in ancient Egypt and was possibly related to the Benu, a bird deity that symbolized the sun and rebirth. But beyond that, descriptions of the phoenix were the subject of some dispute. The bird was either eagle-like in size or larger than an ostrich. Its coloring ranged from brown to peacock-bright, although the fierier shades were particularly popular: glowing red and golden feathers, a purple body, and a rich azure tail, with a tuft of shining feathers on its head and sometimes even a shimmering halo.

As for its famed longevity and regeneration, the Greek historian Herodotus, writing in the fifth century BCE, claimed that the phoenix rose every 500 years at the Temple of the Sun in Heliopolis (Egypt's "City of the Sun"). The Roman historian Tacitus, however, in his *Annals* of the first century CE, was rather more specific in defining the so-called "phoenix period": he declared that it appeared whenever the conventional 365-day calendar aligned exactly with the solar calendar, which is a quarter of a day longer. By his calculation that was every 1,461 years.

There is still no consensus as to the origin of the bird's evocative-sounding name. The Greek *phoinix* could either mean "purple" or refer to Phoenicia, where purple dye was famously produced.

FAWKES IN HARRY POTTER

When faced with the dangerous beasts unleashed by his enemies, Harry Potter knows there is one fearless creature he can rely on to help him: Professor Dumbledore's pet phoenix. It is Fawkes—named after Guy Fawkes, the conspirator who in 1605 tried to blow up England's king and parliament—who helps Harry defeat Salazar Slytherin's basilisk in *The Chamber of Secrets*. Fawkes once gave up two feathers to create powerful wands: one belongs to Harry, the other to Lord Voldemort.

DUAL MEANINGS

Many religious stories have allegorical as well as literal meanings, and so it is with the Dreamtime. (Aptly, "Tjukurrpa" also means "to see and understand the law.") In one popular children's story, the Rainbow Serpent makes deep tracks across the sleeping earth, then wakes the toads and tickles their bellies until water pours out of them, turning its tracks into rivers. It promises to make human all creatures that obey its laws; disobedient subjects are turned into rocks and mountains.

The Rainbow Serpent

A powerful creator-god from deep within the Australian earth, the Rainbow Serpent gives the gift of life—and just as easily takes it away.

I n Christianity the serpent is associated with sin and destruction, but in many Australian Aboriginal traditions, the serpent is the creator-god of the world and everything in it—the bringer of water and life.

The Rainbow Serpent—which in different regions is known by different names, including Wonambi and Wagyl—is intrinsically rooted in the Aboriginal concept of Dreamtime, or "Tjukurrpa": a primitive state that is at once ancient and never-ending, in which the sleeping earth is awakened into creation. As the Rainbow Serpent pushes its way up to the surface, carrying all the slumbering animal families within it, mountains and canyons are created in its wake; its sloughed-off skin forms forests, and where it slithers it carves pathways and riverbeds.

THE WATER OF LIFE

Rainbow Snake myths vary between Aboriginal cultures, some of which see it as female, others as male, but it is commonly associated with water and fertility: in Dreamtime stories, it brings water to the land, allowing new life to flourish. The serpent is thought to inhabit deep waterholes, becoming visible in the sky when it moves from hole to hole; ancient Aboriginal rock paintings dating from up to 8,000 years ago depict the serpent arcing rainbow-like above the Earth. In some traditions, it is only through coming into contact with the serpent's water that young women can become impregnated with "spirit-children." The Rainbow Serpent is thought to be the oldest religious tradition still in existence. The serpent is just as capable of bringing thunder, lightning, and devastating floods as it is the blessing of life-giving rain.

Valkyries

Benevolent Fates or wrathful Furies, the Valkyries have the power to choose who lives, who dies, and who is immortalized as a military hero.

The Fates—or Furies—of Old Norse mythology, Valkyries are charged with choosing which of the soldiers slain in a battle are worthy of being carried to Valhalla, the prestigious "Hall of the Slain" in the afterlife. The name of these formidable female figures, servants of the great god Odin, means "chooser of the slain." In some stories, they do not only transport military heroes to Valhalla: they select which soldiers are doomed to die on the battlefield. They might even choose a favorite soldier to protect from harm.

Valkyries travel as a horde, armed with shields, spears, and helmets, and either ride or fly to the battlefield on horses. The soldiers they choose to take to Valhalla—the *einherjar*, or "former fighters"—spend their time there preparing for Ragnarök, a near-apocalyptic war of the gods billed to happen at some point in the future, while being served mead by the Valkyries.

Both the *Poetic Edda*, a thirteenth-century collection of traditional Norse poems, and the *Prose Edda*, compiled around the same time by the Icelandic historian Snorri Sturluson, contain stories about Valkyries. The number of them riding together at any one time shifts from three to twenty-seven; in some tales they are terrifying to behold while in others they are strikingly beautiful. They are often associated with equally formidable birds: either elegant swans or ominous-looking ravens.

THE RIDE OF THE VALKYRIES

The great German composer Richard Wagner was inspired by Old Norse mythology to write one of his most famous operas, *Die Walküre* (The Valkyrie), the second of four dramas in his celebrated Ring cycle. The epic cycle recounts the life and death of Siegfried, a hero of Norse and Germanic folklore. In *Die Walküre*, which premiered in Munich in 1870, Siegfried's future mother,

VALKYRIE

In the dying months of World War II, Germany's Nazi leadership established a back-up plan in case of a breakdown of civil order and obedience to the cause, codenamed Operation Valkyrie. But with German defeat looking likely by 1944, high-ranking conspirators against Adolf Hitler appropriated the name for their own plot to seize power. The 2008 film *Valkyrie*, starring Tom Cruise, recounts the attempted assassination of Hitler on July 20, 1944; a bomb in a briefcase was detonated during a briefing with the Führer, but he escaped with only scorched trousers. The conspirators were rounded up and executed.

Sieglinde, leaves her husband in order to run away with Siegfried's father, Siegmund. Unbeknownst to them, Siegmund and Sieglinde are the twin children of Wotan, king of the gods, and he plans to ensure their future together. He sends another daughter of his, the Valkyrie Brünnhilde, to guard Siegmund in his duel with Sieglinde's husband, but in the event Wotan changes his mind and Siegmund is slain.

Siegmund's transportation to Valhalla is the theme of the opera's most famous piece: *The Ride of the Valkyries*. Brünnhilde's colleagues arrive amidst a tempestuous storm, and she herself allows the pregnant Sieglinde to escape. To punish Brünnhilde for her disobedience, Wotan makes her mortal; as *Die Walküre* gives way to the next drama in the cycle, he puts her into a deep sleep that only a fearless hero can break—a hero of the calibre of Siegmund's unborn son …

THE VALKYRIES DO NOT ONLY TRANSPORT MILITARY HEROES TO VALHALLA: THEY SELECT WHICH SOLDIERS ARE DOOMED TO DIE ON THE BATTLEFIELD.

PROPHECY AND PERSECUTION

Valkyries are not alone in determining fate in Norse mythology. A more direct counterpart to the Greek Furies are the giant Norns—their name means "secret communicators"—who like the Furies generally work as a trio. Urd, Verdandi, and Skuld (past, present, and future) live in a well beneath the sacred ash tree Yggdrasil, assembly-place of the gods and cradle of the whole universe. Norns traditionally visit newborn babies and influence their fate; while some prophesy misfortune, others bring providence. In the *Prose Edda*, Skuld (future) is included in a list of the Valkyries.

As befits their role as the givers and takers of life, it is the Norns' job to feed Yggdrasil daily with water from the well. Folk stories describe them as either carving people's fates into the bark of the great tree, or weaving fates like a tapestry, much like the Fates of Greek mythology. The Norns have the power to protect someone from death or to condemn him or her to destruction. In one poem from the *Poetic Edda*, a woman is so tormented by the wrathful Norns that she tries to drown herself—only to be washed ashore, alive, to continue to suffer their persecution.

Bibliography

Aeschylus, *Net Fishers*

Aeschylus, *Oresteia* (458 BCE)

Aeschylus, *The Eumenides* (458 BCE)

Apollonius Rhodius, *The Argonautica* (third century BCE)

Bishop Pontoppidan of Bergen, *Natural History of Norway* (1752)

Bram Stoker, *Dracula* (1897)

Brothers Grimm, *Hansel and Gretel* (1812)

Carlo Collodi, *Adventures of Pinocchio* (1883).

Charles Howard-Bury, *Mount Everest: The Reconnaissance* (1921)

Charles Perrault, *Cinderella* (1697)

Charles Perrault, *Histoires ou contes du temps passé* (1697)

Christina Rosetti, *Goblin Market* (poem, 1862)

Clement Clarke Moore, *The Night Before Christmas* (1823)

Compilation of poetry, *Poetic Edda* (c. 800–1100 CE)

Dick King-Smith, *The Water Horse* (1992)

Euripides, *Cyclops* (play)

Euripides, *Orestes* (408 BCE)

Geoffrey of Monmouth, *History of the Kings of Britain* (1136)

Hans Christian Andersen, *The Elf of the Rose* (1839)

Hans Christian Andersen, *The Little Mermaid*, (1837)

Henrik Ibsen, *Peer Gynt* (1867)

Herman Melville, *Moby-Dick*, (1851)

Herminie Templeton Kavanagh, *Darby O'Gill: And the Good People*, (1903)

Hesiod, *Theogony* (poem)

Homer, *Odyssey* (675–725 BCE)

Homer, *Iliad*

J. K. Rowling, *Harry Potter and the Philosopher's Stone* (1997), *Harry Potter and the Chamber of Secrets* (1998), *Harry Potter and the Prisoner of Azkaban* (1999), *Harry Potter and the Goblet of Fire* (2000), *Harry Potter and the Order of the Phoenix* (2003), *Harry Potter and the Half-Blood Prince* (2005), *Harry Potter and the Deathly Hallows* (2007)

J. M. Barrie, *Peter Pan*, (1904), *Peter and Wendy*, (1911)

J. R. R. Tolkien, *The Hobbit* (1937), *The Lord of the Rings* (1954-5)

Jill Murphy, *The Worst Witch* (1974)

Johann Wolfgang von Goethe, *The Fairy King* (poem, 1782)

John Milton, *Paradise Lost* (1667)

John William Polidori, "The Vampyre" (1819)

Kunio Yanagita, *Tono Monogatari* (*Legends of Tono*) (1912)

L. Frank Baum, *Oz* novels (1900-20)

L. Frank Baum, *Wonderful Wizard of Oz* (1900)

Nicolas Flamel, *In Exposition of the Hieroglyphical Figures* (1612)

Ovid, *Metamorphoses* (c.8 BCE) *Ars Amatoria, Heroides* (c.1 BCE)

Peter Christen Asbjørnsen and Jørgen Moe, *Norwegian Folktales* (including *Three Billy Goats Gruff* and *Peer Gynt*) (c.1841)

Pliny the Elder, *Natural History* (77 CE)

Rabbi Moshe Ben Maimon, *Mishneh Torah* (c. 1170)

Roald Dahl, *The Gremlins* (1943), *The BFG* (1982), *The Witches* (1983)

Seán mac Ruaidhri Mac Craith, *Cathreim Thoirdhealbhaigh*, or *Triumphs of Turlough*

Sir Arthur Conan Doyle, *The Coming of the Fairies* (1922)

Snorri Sturluson, *Prose Edda* (c. 1220)

Sophocles, *Icheutnae* (play)

Story compilation, *The Thousand and One Nights* (1717)

Tacitus, *Annals*, (first century CE)

The Beowulf Poet, *Beowulf* (c.1000)

The Bible

The Book of the Dead (Egyptian) (1550 BCE)

The Brothers Grimm, *Snow White and the Seven Dwarfs* (1812)

The Quran

The Story of Jack Spriggins and the Enchanted Bean (1734)

Tibetan Book of the Dead (1326–1386)

Virgil, *Aeneid* (c. 30 BCE), *Eclogues* (c. 40 BCE)

W. B. Yeats, *Fairy and Folk Tales of the Irish Peasantry* (1888)

While C. S. Lewis, *The Chronicles of Narnia* (1950–1956)

William Allingham, *The Lepracaun* (poem)

William Seabrook, *The Magic Island* (1929)

William Shakespeare, *A Midsummer Night's Dream* (c.1595), *Macbeth* (c.1600)

William Steig, *Shrek!* (1990)

Glossary

Abrahamic religions: Religions with a common reverence for the patriarch Abraham. The three major Abrahamic religions, in order of establishment, are Judaism, Christianity, and Islam.

Afterlife: The life that follows death in the beliefs of many cultures, ancient and modern.

Ancient Egypt: A term used to describe the civilization that flourished in Egypt between the fourth and first millennia BCE. Ruled over by pharaohs, the ancient Egyptians are best known for their imposing pyramids and their practice of mummifying corpses before burial.

BCE: Before the Common Era (also known as BC: Before Christ). The time before the year 0, associated by Christians with the birth of Jesus Christ.

Bible: A collection of sacred texts most commonly associated with Christianity, although the Old Testament is taken from the earlier Hebrew Bible. The New Testament, unique to Christianity, relates the birth, life, and works of Jesus Christ.

Brothers Grimm: German brothers Jacob and Wilhelm, who collected and published a collection of European folk tales in the nineteenth century.

CE: Common Era (also known as AD: Anno Domini, "in the year of the Lord"). The time after the year 0, associated by Christians with the birth of Jesus Christ.

Dreamtime or the Dreaming: In Australian Aboriginal mythology, the period in which everything was, is, and will continue to be awakened into creation. Dreamtime is both ancient and never-ending.

Fates, The: In Greek mythology, three goddesses who determined a person's destiny. Clotho would spin the thread of life, Lachesis would measure out the length accorded to each person, and Atropos would cut it when the allotted time was up.

Folklore: The traditional beliefs, myths, tales, and customs of a community, handed down through storytelling.

Germanic or Norse mythology: The system of religious, mythological, and philosophical beliefs that was prevalent in Northern European German-speaking lands—including Scandinavia and England—before their conversion to Christianity. The pantheon of Germanic gods was headed by Odin, to whose palace, Valhalla, the Valkyries transported slain battlefield heroes.

Greek mythology: The system of religious, mythological, and philosophical beliefs that was prevalent in ancient Greece, a civilization that lasted from around 1200 BCE until the fourth century CE. The pantheon of Greek gods—who were believed to live on Mount Olympus—was headed by Zeus. One of his sons, Hercules, was a great military hero who fell into disgrace; as punishment, he was dispatched by King Eurystheus to perform a series of seemingly impossible tasks—The Twelve Labors of Hercules—most of which involved mortal combat with fearsome mythological beasts.

Homer: Greek poet believed to have lived and worked in around the eighth century BCE. He is credited with writing the *Iliad*, an epic poem about the Trojan War, and the *Odyssey*, an account of the Greek hero Odysseus's ten-year voyage home from that conflict. On his journey, Odysseus encounters a series of monstrous creatures, including the Cyclopes and the Sirens.

Middle Ages: The period of history dating from roughly 500 to 1500 CE, often described as the "medieval" period.

Philosopher's Stone: A magical substance that was believed to cure all diseases, guarantee immortality, and turn worthless metals into gold, which alchemists (or wizards) of the sixteenth and seventeenth centuries were determined to obtain or create.

***Poetic Edda* and *Prose Edda*:** The former is a thirteenth-century compilation of Old Norse poems, and the latter a comprehensive history of Old Norse

Index

acknowledgments

This book was conceived, designed, and produced by
Quantum Books Ltd.

Publisher: Kerry Enzor
Managing Editor: Julia Shone
Editorial: Emma Harverson
Designer: Lucy Parissi
Illustrator: Andrew Pinder
Production Manager: Zarni Win

Thanks also to Silvia Crompton, Nicky Hill, Lindsay Kaubi, Rachel Malig, Anna
Southgate, and Vanessa Bird for their editorial work and index.